ALEX KO

ALEX KO

From Iowa to Broadway
My BILLY ELLIOT Story

By Alex Ko

HARPER
An Imprint of HarperCollins*Publishers*

Lyrics on pages 144–145, page 146, and the jacket by Elton John and Lee Hall. Reprinted with permission from Universal Pictures Stage Productions and Working Title.

www.harpercollinschildrens.com

Library of Congress Control Number: 2013932626
ISBN 978-0-06-223601-2 (trade bdg.)

Typography by Tom Starace
13 14 15 16 17 LP/RRDH 10 9 8 7 6 5 4 3 2 1
❖

First Edition

You taught me how to walk, ride my bike,

catch fish, and most of all to Believe. . . .

This is for you, Dad.

I love you.

Contents

Introduction

It wasn't until the stage manager yelled "thirty minutes" that it really hit me: I was about to star in a Broadway show. Right outside my dressing room door, fifteen hundred people were waiting. I was thirteen years old and I'd spent my whole life in Iowa, so the idea of performing for an audience that size was surreal. I could barely believe it was happening.

Maybe I should have been scared, but mostly I was excited (and a little nervous). I was playing the lead in *Billy Elliot*, a musical about a poor British boy who desperately wants to be a ballet dancer. It's a great show, and if you haven't seen it, you should definitely rent the movie.

As I practiced my lines in my head, I thought about how much I had in common with Billy. We were almost the exact same age, we'd both lost one of our parents, and we both loved dancing. In fact, I took my first dance class when I was four, which I guess is weird for a boy. But my older brother had taken tap lessons, and I wanted to be just like him. And guess what.

I hated it.

Even though I loved dancing, I hated the way everyone stared at me as the new kid. I wouldn't dance at all—I wouldn't even stand up! I sat on my hands for the entire class, and I refused to go back. Thankfully, I got over that.

While the orchestra tuned up and the audience found their seats, I waited in my dressing room on the second floor of the Imperial Theatre, the same place where *Les Misérables*, *Fiddler on the Roof*, and *The Boy from Oz* were staged. It's hard not to feel humble when you're sharing a stage with the echoes of some of the biggest names in show business, like Ben Vereen and Hugh Jackman. Legends were made in this theater. The more I thought about it, the more I worried: what if I forgot a line or tripped? Fifteen hundred people, including just about everyone I knew in the whole world, would be watching. I was going to be singing music written by Elton John! I had to be perfect. I sat on my hands to keep myself from fidgeting and tried to run my lines. Stephen Daldry, the show's director, had me rehearse all day in order to keep me distracted. But now I was alone, and I could hear the crowd gathering. A chorus of worries was singing in my head. I turned on my iPod and put on Lady Gaga to drown them out.

Over the music, I heard a knock on the door.

"Almost ready?" said Jess, my dresser, as she peeked her head in.

I nodded, relieved to see her. Without Jess Scoblick, I would never have been able to do the show. I wore so many outfits and had to change between them so fast, there was no way I could do it all on my own. Sometimes I had only a few seconds to switch from one costume to the next. For my first scene, I had to wear three outfits one on top of the other so I could do really quick changes. Jess helped me pull on boxing shorts, then put pajamas on over the shorts, and then put track pants and a jacket over all of that. It was like being a little kid bundled up for a snowstorm—except that I had to be able to dance while wearing all of it!

Jess was the best dresser anyone could ever have. She took care of me and became a great friend. During rehearsals, she was always boosting my spirits and helping me feel confident.

"You're gonna be great," she said as she fixed the collar on my jacket and straightened my shirt. Her long dark hair framed her almost-always-smiling face.

"Thanks," I said. Somewhere in the distance, a loudspeaker announced our fifteen-minute call. Jess left, but before the door could close, Stephen, the director, came in. He was tall and gray-haired, with a British accent that I tried to mimic when I played Billy.

"There's one more thing you need to do," he said, and took me downstairs. I couldn't imagine what it was. Could there be any part of the play I hadn't already rehearsed earlier that day? But Stephen had become like a godfather to me, so I knew if there was something he wanted me to do, it was for a good reason.

Backstage was a whirl of crew and scenery and costumes. It's incredible how many people it takes to run a Broadway show. Tonight was extra busy because there were two of us making our debuts—me and Kate Hennig, the actor who played my dance teacher. It was nice having someone else around who was still learning the ropes, but it made opening night all the more chaotic. Stephen and I had to dodge around people on our way down to the main stage. And the whole time, I couldn't take my eyes off the heavy red velvet curtain that separated us from the audience. Very, very soon, it would go up, and the show would begin. I would be on Broadway!

"Told you I'd find him," Stephen said as he opened

the stage door and let my mom in. He winked at me and hurried off.

"I didn't think I'd see you before the show!" I said as Mom hugged me. She smelled like home, which right then seemed very far away.

My mom is one of the most amazing people I know. I wouldn't even be a dancer, let alone on Broadway, if not for her. But one of the best things about her is that she isn't a "stage mom." She's not one of those parents who hover around their kids at every audition, pampering them and driving everyone else crazy. She trusts me to be responsible. So I was surprised that she came by—surprised, and really happy.

"I told you I'd come by before you went on," she said. She smiled and fixed my hair. "I didn't know if they'd let me in, but Stephen made it happen. You're going to be great tonight. I love you."

I didn't know what to say, so I hugged her again, and she ran back to find her seat before the curtain went up. Seeing her gave me the boost I needed to get over my nerves. Now I just wanted to go out onstage. There were only a few minutes before the show started, and everyone was taking their places. I hurried to find my mark.

But suddenly I heard Stephen talking to the audience. For some reason, he was out in front of that heavy velvet curtain giving a speech. That's definitely not the way the show usually starts, so I strained my ears and listened.

"He is without question one of the greatest dancers in the country," I heard Stephen say. It took me a moment to realize he was talking about me! In fact, he said great things about everyone in the cast, especially Kate and me (since we were new). I just hoped I could live up to his words.

When he was finished, the audience applauded and then hushed. After a long time (or maybe two more minutes—I couldn't tell), the show finally started. One by one, the members of the ensemble filed past me. I heard "break a leg" as they went, dark silhouettes disappearing onto the bright stage one after another.

When the moment came for my grand Broadway entrance, I lowered my head, took a deep breath, and got dragged onto the stage. That's right: my first time on Broadway and someone was already dragging me around!

In my first scene, my "dad" is upset and he pulls me out onto the stage with him. I was supposed to stare at the ground while he yelled. But I couldn't help myself: I broke character and peeked. Who wouldn't? This was my moment. I wanted to remember every detail: the way the audience looked, how the lights felt on my skin, the scratchy floor sliding beneath me. I tried to be as subtle as I could without missing a thing.

The view from the stage is strange, just a lot of indistinct shadows and bright lights. I wanted to look at the whole theater, but I could only move my head so far without anyone noticing. But there in the front row was Eloy Barragan, one of my ballet teachers. As though I needed more pressure! My eyes searched the audience, looking for other familiar faces, but I found none. For all I could tell, the theater was filled with cardboard cutouts.

Then I saw the lined face of the tall, gray-haired conductor, and it hit me.

Whoa, I thought. *This is real.*

I don't know why seeing the conductor made me realize that. Maybe it's because in normal life you only see the back of the conductor's head. But seeing his face let me know that I wasn't dreaming. It was October 6, 2009, and in a few seconds I'd say my first line in a real Broadway show. I tried to prepare myself. I thought of my family in the audience, all the people who loved me but couldn't be there, and God. Then I took a deep breath, opened my mouth, and said: "It's to do with Maggie Thatcher, isn't it?"

The next thing I knew, the show was over and the audience was giving me a standing ovation. That's how it is for me when I'm onstage. I would never say that being a performer is easy. It's one of the hardest things I can imagine doing. But all the work happens offstage, in classes, rehearsals, and auditions. For every hour of performing, there are weeks—sometimes even months—of preparation. And it can be really hard work, filled with long hours, bad injuries, and endless repetition. But when you're onstage, you never let that show. You relax and just . . . be. At least, that's what I do. That night, I *was* Billy Elliot—and it was great.

Seeing all those people stand up and applaud was amazing, especially because my mom, and my brothers, John and Matt, were there. In fact, almost my entire extended family had come to see the show, along with half of Iowa (or at least it felt that way). Even my great-grandma was there, and she never traveled on a plane.

Originally, I hadn't wanted my family to come to my first performance, because I always worry the most about what they think. I wanted to be perfect by the time they saw the show. But once the performance was over, I couldn't wait to see them.

I wished my dad could have been there. He had died two years earlier, when I was eleven. Billy lost his mom when he was ten. But he still talks to his mom all the time, the same way I do with my dad. Every night before

I go to bed, I tell him everything that's happened that day. Tonight, I would have lots to say.

Like Billy's dad, my father had a hard time with me being a dancer. He didn't think it was serious, and he wanted me to focus on more respectable things, like becoming a doctor. But when I showed him how much I loved it, he became the most supportive father you could imagine. In fact, he's the one who pushed me toward ballet. Though I wished he could have been there that night, I knew he had the best seat in the house, up in heaven.

After my final bow, the curtain closed for good—but the applause didn't stop. The whole cast and crew of the show were applauding for Kate and me, because it was our first night. Jess and Stephen both swept me up in congratulatory hugs. From the stagehands to the ballet girls, everyone was excited to see us do well. There was a giant circle of people around me applauding. I looked around the room and thought, *I want to do this forever.*

Little did I know that eight days later I would be out of the show, and possibly never dance again.

I guess I should start at the beginning. . . .

How I Almost Never Learned to Dance

The first stage I ever performed on was the hardwood floor of my family's living room in Iowa City, Iowa. I was a four-year-old dance prodigy, choreographing elaborate shows with a full orchestra, an army of backup dancers, and an audience of thousands.

Okay, I'd never taken a dance class, the orchestra was on tape, my only backup dancer was my dog Ming Ming, and the "audience" was my family. But as my bare feet slid across our living room floor in uncoordinated attempts at pirouettes and handsprings, I felt like a star. This was what I was born to do.

No, not dance in my living room. Perform. I never

dreamed that I would make it as far as I have, but I always knew I'd be a dancer, no matter what. It was just in me, in my blood, from the moment I was born.

I used to spend all day getting ready for my "shows." My dad, Sam Ko, was born in Hong Kong, which meant he had a nifty British accent *and* a lot of CDs and DVDs of Chinese pop songs (it also makes me Chinese American, since my mom, Tammie, is from Florida). Whenever we went to Chicago, Dad would go to Chinatown to buy music. On the way back home, I'd sit in the back of the car and listen to those out-of-this-world sounds. When we got home, I obsessively watched the DVDs, which were filled with kaleidoscopic colors and beautiful women in neon dance clubs. They were like nothing I ever saw on TV in Iowa City. We didn't even have cable, let alone videos from around the world. They were my escape from our normal suburban life, into a world of excitement and magic—the world of theater, where anything was possible.

Maybe that sounds childish, but it's exactly what I thought when I was four: that theater could take me out of this world and into a whole new one. Or into a dozen new ones. Or a million.

And I was right.

I loved those songs, even though I couldn't understand a word of Chinese. Maybe, actually, that's why I loved them. Nothing got in the way of feeling the music. I would close my eyes and move, without caring what I looked like. There's that old saying "dance as though no one's watching," and that's what I did every day. Sometimes I would imagine a perfect world—not anything in particular, but the feeling of being somewhere free and perfect and wonderful. I would try to move in a way that expressed how I felt. I would leap and flip and jump, hop and step and kick. I'd mimic the dancers and gymnasts I saw on TV, long before I actually knew how to do any of the moves.

Mom says that I was "energetic" and "creative" (which is mom-speak for "wild" and "stubborn"). Dancing was a great way for me to get all of my energy out without constantly being in her way.

Not that performing in the living room was particularly "out of the way." Sometimes, if I was really going crazy, Dad would chase me around the house with a rolled-up newspaper, and I would run from him, laughing. "You're going to be a top surgeon," he would say when he caught me. He'd carefully take my hands and tell me that they were the "hands of great surgeon!" But then he'd soften up. "But if you really want, maybe an actor," he'd add. "The next Robert De Niro, that's you." He would smile wide and shake his head with pride.

"I always knew you were going to do important things with your life," Mom says now. Not because I danced all the time, though I did, but because of what I did afterward. I made her tape all of my shows, and when I finished performing, I sat in my room and studied the tapes over and over again. I needed to know what I could do better. I analyzed every step, every kick, every turn. I wanted to be perfect, because even then I knew that's what it took to be an actor, or a dancer, or any kind of artist.

It's embarrassing to watch those tapes now and see my bowl-cut hair flying and my arms flailing. If you saw me then, you'd be *really* surprised I ever made it to Broadway. But there's no way you could miss the giant smile on my face. I loved dancing, and I always have.

"Alex!" Dad would say when I'd spent too many hours poring over the videos trying to improve my footwork. "Come on—we're going for a bike ride."

Dad and I used to bike everywhere: up and down Teg Drive, the quiet suburban street we lived on; out to the University of Iowa, where I would stare at the white stone buildings and dream about going to college; or my favorite, over to the nearby reservoir, where we would go fishing. Together with my older brother, John, and our younger brother, Matt, we'd spend long summer afternoons on the banks. Fishing was just an excuse to hang out. We'd wrestle and fight and swim. On the way home, I'd stand on the back of John's bike and feel the wind rushing all around me. It felt like flying.

I spent a lot of time with my brothers and my dad when I was little. Dad took care of the house, while Mom worked for the ACT, that test that high school seniors take to get into college. My mom's really smart. Like, *for-real* smart. She has a PhD in applied statistics and psychometrics, which basically means math. Really hard math.

It's probably weird to some people that my dad stayed home while my mom worked. But it was the right thing for our family. It showed me from an early age that what mattered most was doing what was right for you, not what anyone else said was right. It was a lesson that really helped during the long years when I was the only boy in any of my dance classes. If you're a guy, and you want to dance, be prepared. Most of the time, you'll be the only one. But you'll always stand out, and for a performer, that's a good thing.

I was lucky—not many people in our neighborhood judged us in any way. Iowa City was a great, open-minded place to grow up, and our neighborhood had a real community feel. People were accepting of all kinds of different folks.

Dad did lots of things around the house (he even built the speakers I used for my shows), but he was an especially great cook. Before I was born, his family owned a Chinese restaurant in Iowa City. In fact, that's where he met my mom. In 1993, the Mississippi and Missouri Rivers both flooded, leaving thirty thousand square miles of the country underwater. It was one of the worst natural disasters to ever hit America. My dad was living in California, but he came to Iowa to help his sisters get their restaurant back together after the flood nearly destroyed it. My mom just happened to work there. It sounds like the plot of a musical, doesn't it? A big disaster, a new boss with an exotic accent, and a beautiful girl who was waiting tables to pay for college. It's no wonder Dad loved to cook after that!

While I played his Chinese pop tapes, Dad would be in the kitchen, whipping up big pots of noodles and dumplings. He cooked for us every day. I can't have Chinese food now without missing him.

Things were pretty great until I turned five, when it was time to go to school. School and I didn't get along. At all.

I don't want to give anyone the wrong idea: I love

learning, and I plan on going to college at Yale. Or maybe Stanford. A good school, regardless. But elementary school was hard. When I wasn't home or performing, I was really shy. As a character in a show, I could say the craziest things. And I've always been able to express my feelings through dance. But making friends at school was difficult. The teachers said I was smart but needed to stay focused. At home, we had lots of rules and chores we had to do around the house, but the rest of the time my family let me go at my own pace. At school, everything was much more structured. I had so much energy that I just couldn't sit still. My kindergarten teacher told my parents that I kept doing other students' work for them, to hurry things along. I mostly spent recess alone, wandering the playground and kicking piles of snow. I was always that kid who got along better with my teachers than my classmates.

I had only one close friend, and we weren't even in the same school. His name was Sasha Trouch, and he was Russian. Our moms had been friends for years, so I'd known him basically my whole life. His house was just a five-minute bike ride away. Maybe part of the reason we got along is that both of our families were pretty different from everyone else around us. Eventually, his dad, Dmitri, would become one of my first important mentors.

If you've seen *Billy Elliot*, you know that he had only one good friend too, a boy named Michael. It was one of the many things Billy and I had in common, which I think is a big part of the reason I was able to play the role as well as I did. So I guess in the long run, it was all good. But when I was a kid, school made me feel lonely. I couldn't wait for the bell to ring so I could rush home.

Both my parents believed that schooling was the number one priority in life. My great-grandma always told me that my education was the one thing no one could ever take from me. So when I had problems in public school, my parents tried everything they could think of: first homeschooling, then back to public school, then to private school, then back to homeschooling. . . . I bounced around a bit during those first few years.

Even while I was in kindergarten, my parents were desperate to find something to keep my mind off my school troubles, so right when I started school, they took me to a gymnastics class. For once, all the adults in the room were telling me to get up and run around. Maybe because I wasn't the only boy, I loved it from the very first day. We were free to run, and move, and jump. It was like all that energy I had to force down in school could finally come rushing out. And I was a pretty quick study. We've even got a video of me doing a front handspring in one of my Chinese pop "shows" when I was just six years old.

Soon I was going to gymnastics three or four times a week, and Sasha was in every class with me. My mom would pick us up from school and bring us home from the gym. Sasha's mom, Marina, made my dance costumes. My little brother, Matt, even joined the team, and soon we were competing together. Our two families became really close. Some days, we'd hang out at Sasha's place so late playing video games that I would have to call home and spend the night. If you added it all up, we probably spent months of our lives at each other's houses.

One day, after watching me in a competition, Marina asked if I'd like to train with her husband, Dmitri, who was then working at the University of Iowa as a coach with the men's gymnastics team.

"Alex has real potential," Marina told my mom.

I was really excited to train with Dmitri, because the university had one of the best college teams in the country. But it wasn't until later that Sasha told me the whole truth: before he'd come to Iowa, his dad had been an Olympic gymnast in Russia. In 1996, he won a Gold Medal at the Summer Olympics in Atlanta! Dmitri was so humble, he never bragged about his achievements at all. But I was honored that he wanted to train me.

By the time I was eight, I was going to gymnastics every day, and sometimes weekends too. We shared the gym with students from the Hawkeye gymnastics team. Sometimes they gave us tips, mostly on the small things that make a huge difference in your score in competition, like remembering to point your toes. I promised myself that one day I'd be just as good as any of them.

At home, Matt and I festooned our shared bedroom with plaques and trophies from gymnastics. The back of our door was strung with dozens of ribbons. We might not have been as good as those college gymnasts, but when I closed my eyes at night, I could see myself wearing the Hawkeye uniform someday.

But what I really wanted was to be as good as Dmitri. I could just imagine myself standing on that Olympic platform wearing red, white, and blue, and listening to the loudspeaker announce my name while the national anthem played.

And if it hadn't been for one little incident, I think I might have made it. . . .

Missteps

I wiped the sweat from my brow and stared at the parallel bars (or p-bars, as we called them). Even though the gym was about a thousand degrees, I was wearing long pants. Normally, we worked out in shorts, but for certain pieces of equipment, like p-bars, we wore pants to protect ourselves.

"Come on, Alex," said Coach. "Again! I'll spot you."

Coach had a thick, aggressive European accent, so pretty much everything he said sounded stern. Then again, pretty much everything he said *was* stern. Some students disliked him for it, but I appreciated how much he pushed us. I hate it when adults assume I can't take something seriously just because I'm young, or when they lie to "protect" me. I'd always rather know the truth, and Coach never held back. . . .

To prepare for getting back on the p-bars, I rubbed fresh chalk onto my hands, which were already sore from an intense workout. Our training sessions were three to four hours long. From the moment we walked in the door to the second we ran gratefully out into the cold night air, Coach worked us. If we were even a minute late, he would make us climb the rope ten times. The ceiling was a good fifty feet up. By the time we were done climbing, our arms and abs burned. And that was before we started warming up, which included push-ups, running, and hundreds of sit-ups. Only then would we actually practice our events!

Even though it was only February, I was already contacting special summer programs for Olympic hopefuls, because that's how seriously I took gymnastics. Coach and I were working on a double pirouette, which is when you do a handstand on the bar and then spin around in a circle, shifting your weight carefully so you stay absolutely straight the entire time. The one little complication? You do it all one-handed. I was determined to get it right.

"Up!" Coach said, and clapped his burly hands. I positioned myself between the bars and piked up to a handstand. Tiny drops of sweat covered my chest and mixed with the chalk dust to form a layer of slick gray mud all over my body.

Maybe it was the sweat that did it. Maybe my hands were slippery or my arms were just tired from the workout. But as I put all my weight onto my right side and began my pirouette, my arm buckled. I tried to straighten out, to keep my bones stacked neatly so that I wasn't depending on just my muscles to hold me up, but it was no use.

"Alex!" I heard Coach yell as I tumbled on top of him. His hands grabbed me, trying to guide me gently to the ground, but I was moving too fast. I careened into the equipment. My right leg slammed hard into the p-bars, and I yelled.

This wasn't the first time I'd fallen off a piece of equipment. Accidents are a part of life for any athlete, and I'd even broken a finger once before. But right away I could tell this was different. It hurt like my leg had been immersed in boiling water.

"Are you okay?" Coach asked. We were sitting on the ground, though I didn't remember getting there.

I gritted my teeth and nodded. "I'm fine, Coach."

"Training isn't over!" Coach snapped, sending everyone running back to their equipment. He peeled away the bottom part of my pant leg to reveal a bloody, bruised mess where my right shin used to be. It felt inflamed, like there was a hot-water balloon right beneath my skin. Coach sent an assistant for an ice pack and carefully helped me clean the cut.

"It's okay," he assured me. "It's good for you to get through this. Gymnastics is all about working through the pain."

That might sound crazy to some people, but pain is part of the game. Coach always reminded us about Kerri Strug, who tore two ligaments while vaulting at the '96 Olympics but continued competing until she literally collapsed. Her team won a Gold Medal thanks to her dedication. Endurance was a virtue we had drilled into us—and one that would come back to haunt me as a dancer years from now.

So I told Coach I was fine, and he let me sit out the last few minutes of the session. I spent it holding the ice pack to my leg, trying to will the swelling to go down.

And that's when I made a big mistake.

Instead of calling my mom and going to the doctor immediately, I tried to hide it. While everyone else headed to the lockers, I squinted my eyes, looked at my leg, and decided it wasn't that bad.

"Work through the pain," I whispered.

Even though gymnastics was my main focus, I was still dancing pretty regularly. I wanted to be an Olympian, but dance . . . dance made my soul sing. I couldn't imagine a life without it. I had to fit it in around my training schedule, though, so I often went right from one workout to another. By the end of the day, I was always exhausted, but I told myself that doing one helped the other. Dancing worked my rhythm, endurance, and balance, while gymnastics pushed my strength and flexibility. Everyone told me I had to focus on something, but I wanted to do it all.

The next day, dance class was a mess. My teacher could tell instantly that I was injured and called my mom. By the time I got home, my shin looked like it had a giant purple football attached to it.

"You're not going to the Invitational," Mom said. The Invitational was our next big meet, the one I'd been training for all month. I knew the look on her face. It was the one that said arguing would get me nowhere.

"But—" I couldn't help it. My team was depending on me.

"No," said Mom, and I knew there was no way I was going.

Or at least, there was no way I was competing. But because Matt and I were on the same team, I begged her to let me go watch.

"It'll boost morale to have Alex there," Coach told my

mom. "And we won't put him up."

The doctor said I had a fracture, but that it would heal normally if I took care of it and didn't do anything. I was frustrated. Just walking on my leg hurt! And I didn't want my career as a gymnast to end before I was even in my teens. So I gritted my teeth, took the doctor's advice, and did nothing.

It was the worst week ever.

By the time we got to Minnesota, I was totally psyched to win. There was a good chance that we might walk away with individual *and* team awards.

I had to keep reminding myself that I'd only be cheering this time. I tried not to worry about my injury, or how not competing would look to the Olympic training programs. I needed time to heal. Worrying about things beyond my control was a quick road to crazy town. This was an important lesson my parents and my church had taught me: take care of the things you can take care of. Leave the rest to God.

I just hoped that God wanted me to go to the Olympics too.

"Good luck!" Mom said as we entered the gym. She gave Matt a big hug, then turned to me. "You sure you don't want to sit with me?"

I shook my head. I wanted to be as close to the action

as possible. She headed up to find her seat in the bleachers, while Matt and I went down to the floor.

"Race you!" Matt said, when he spotted our teammates. I pointed to my leg.

"Guess I win!" He smiled.

As soon as I'm better . . . I thought.

It was just one more reminder that I wasn't competing. Talk about a total bummer. Thankfully, the entire team was in a great mood, and they kept my spirits up as the day went on.

"Next time, I get to sit on the bench and relax," joked Matt as he went to do his pommel-horse routine. I smiled, but I would have given anything to switch places with him.

In event after event, our team did really well. It was clear that we were one of the ones to watch.

Why did I have to be injured for this competition, of all competitions? I thought. It was so unfair. God has a reason for everything, but sometimes those reasons are *really* hard to understand.

The competition was down to the last few events when I noticed Coach staring at me. As I watched, he waved the meet director over. They whispered to each other for a few seconds. Coach looked down at his score sheet. Then he came over to me.

"Warm up," he said.

"But, Coach, I'm not—" I protested.

"The team needs you," he said firmly. "The vault. Get ready."

Then he walked away.

It would be an understatement to say that I had no idea what to do. I desperately wanted to compete, and if I scored well, there was a chance our team could take first place. Plus, in gymnastics, you do what your coach says. But the doctor had told me to lay off my leg completely, and I knew Mom would go through the roof when she saw me compete.

"Alex!" called out Coach. "Hurry up."

What could I do? I knew it was wrong, but I started stretching.

The swelling in my leg had gone down, but there was still a big purple lump on my shin, and it hurt when I did too much. But the team was depending on me.

"Work through the pain," I told myself as I practiced my splits. "Work through the pain."

The vault was my best event, hands down. I was little for my age, and I could flip over the vaulting table like I'd been launched from a slingshot. And, I told myself, it wasn't like I was doing floor work, which was *really* tough on my shin.

But what about your landing? a little voice whispered in my head. *How's your leg gonna handle that?*

I was planning a front handspring vault, a move with which I was very familiar. It was difficult, but I could land it. I felt the excitement rushing through me. By the time I stepped up to the vault, my leg didn't hurt at all.

At least, I didn't *feel* any pain. As I threw myself into my move, my leg didn't even twitch. I hit my handspring perfectly.

Yes! I thought. I'd made the right decision. Coach and the team would be proud, and Mom and my doctor would understand.

Then I hit the ground.

I had so much adrenaline in my system that I didn't feel anything other than a weird weakness. For some reason, my right leg wouldn't hold up, as though it were made of paper. I prided myself on always sticking my landings, but I couldn't help it. In order to keep from falling over, I had to hop once—a definite deduction from my score. Thankfully, when I landed the second time, my leg didn't betray me. It was a great vault, not perfect, but my body knew the move well.

Then Coach asked me to do my floor routine—something my leg definitely wasn't ready for. But it was my second-best event, and I'd done well on the vault, so . . .

I did it.

I started off strong, but my leg couldn't hold. After I completed my most difficult pass, I couldn't stop. My leg felt like it would collapse if I tried to stand still, so *hop, hop, hop* I went. After the third hop, I finally got my leg to hold up. It was far from the best floor routine I'd ever done, but I hoped it would be enough to put my team in first place. Then I looked down at the ground, and my heart sank.

I had crossed the fault line. Automatic deduction for going out of bounds. That had never happened to me—ever. There went our chances of winning.

And that's when the pain came back. I think I blacked out a little, because the next thing I remember seeing was Mom, who had raced down to the floor. Parents aren't allowed near the athletes, so she couldn't get to me, or to any of the coaches on our team.

"Alex!" she yelled. "Are you all right?"

I nodded. I was pretty sure I hadn't done any real damage, but I was embarrassed and ashamed. I'd wanted to win, and I'd put that before my own health. I was all set for her to yell at me.

But instead, she turned on my coaches. I don't know if I'd ever seen her that upset or scared. She was always the calm, rational one. But not that day. I almost felt bad for Coach! Then she called Dmitri on his cell. He wasn't at the meet because he was coaching the big boys (that's what we called the University of Iowa's men's team). Dmitri agreed with her that I shouldn't have been competing. Though it made him really sad, he understood why she had to do what she did next.

"No more," she said to me, after the medics had looked at my leg. "You could have been seriously injured—even paralyzed. You're not doing gymnastics anymore."

This time, I didn't argue. I knew it would get me nowhere. And more than that, she was right. Gymnastics was a dangerous sport, and even though I loved Dmitri and my team, I needed to take care of myself.

I don't fault anyone for what happened (other than myself)—that's just the way the sport is. You have to love it enough to give it everything. When my leg collapsed beneath me, I realized: I didn't love gymnastics enough.

Luckily, I'd found something I really did love.

My Return to Dance

Even though I hadn't enjoyed my first dance class, I kept making tapes of myself dancing. Soon the tapes began to pile up in my closet. By the time I was five—a year after I'd gone to that first, disastrous dance class—I had quite a collection of them.

My older brother, John, was ten, and for a couple of years he'd been taking classes with a woman named Michael Kohli, who ran a school called the National Dance Academy. It was the big-deal competition dance school in Iowa City. It had bright, airy studios and these beautiful swooping chandeliers in the lobby. They had thousands of crystals hanging from them. They looked . . . *expensive*. Every day I'd sit and count the crystals while

Mom and I waited for John to finish class. It felt like the most elegant place in the world, like I'd already left Iowa and was sitting in the lobby of a Broadway theater—not that I'd ever even been to Broadway at that point in my life, but I could dream.

Mom knew I loved dancing. *And* she knew I needed something to do with all my pent-up energy. *And* John was already going to this studio, so . . . she decided to do something totally underhanded and unfair.

Without telling me, she took one of my dancing tapes and gave it to Michael, John's teacher, who loved it. The next time we dropped John off at the studio, I found myself enrolled in a dance class.

"He has natural talent," Michael told my mom.

I was *mortified* that she had seen the tape, mainly because of one small detail: I wasn't wearing a lot in the video. In fact, I was in my underwear! I was so mad at Mom that I refused to talk to her the entire way home.

But being with John helped me overcome my shyness. Plus Michael was the best teacher a young dancer could have. She had a beautiful smile, and had trained in New York City before opening her studio in Iowa in the early 1980s. She had a huge amount of experience, and she knew how to make class fun.

I took all kinds of classes from her: jazz, modern,

lyrical, improv. Pretty much anything they taught at the National Dance Academy, I studied. (Ironically, the only two classes I didn't take much of with Michael were tap and ballet—the two things I would need for *Billy Elliot*!) The studio became my second home. I spent a little more time in the gym doing gymnastics, but that was more competitive. Dance was just . . . joyful.

You have to look for your joy. To be successful at something like dance takes a huge amount of work. You dedicate your life to it. And if you dedicate your life to something that doesn't bring you joy, well . . . that sounds pretty miserable, doesn't it? Dad always said that the only thing to be ashamed of in life is not doing your very best, and it's easier to do your best when you love what you're doing.

Most of what I did with Michael was competition dancing. This meant that we focused more on performance than technique, though we did both. Over the six or seven years I studied with her, I danced in something like fifty competitions, which were held all across the country. At each one, I performed anywhere from one to ten numbers—some solos, some duos, and some big group performances. That's literally hundreds of dances. And all of those dances were made of moves and combinations that I had to learn first. It took hours and hours of classes and rehearsals in order to be able to compete.

Mom drove me to everything, and dancing was the way we bonded. She was never a dancer herself, like my auntie Kristin, but my mom could see how much I loved it, and wanted to support me. Without fail, she came to every dance competition and recital.

Which felt really good, because Dad . . . Dad wasn't as into me being a dancer. He wanted me to be a surgeon, or a gymnast, or even an actor.

"Jumping up and down!" he'd huff when he saw me rehearsing at home. "That's not dance! It's aerobics."

I'd be lying if I said it didn't hurt. I wanted Dad to be proud of me, and he was—when it came to everything else. But he didn't think dance was serious. He was scared I was wasting my talents. He was so against it, he never came to a single competition.

"Alex, he's just worried for you," Mom said, when I'd ask why he didn't come.

I knew she was right, but still . . . I always dreamed of the day when he would see me dance and realize that this was the thing I was born to do. That this was my passion. Just like in *Billy Elliot*, the more Dad disliked my dancing, the more I wanted to make him proud of it. I thought if I just worked hard enough, someday he would see it.

But it seemed like he would never understand my passion for dance.

In the meantime, dance was something Mom and I bonded over. There's a lot of work that goes into making a dance. I wanted to be involved in every aspect. One of my favorite things to do was help make my costumes. Dance costumes are fitted and stretchy so you can move in them, but they're also bright and beautiful to catch the judges' attention. They're like what ice skaters wear in the Olympics. I loved picking out colors and patterns that helped tell the story of my dance.

Plus it didn't hurt that I was really into the Power Rangers at the time, who just happened to wear bright, stretchy costumes to battle evil. I'm not saying that was my *main* reason for wanting to help make the costumes, but it certainly didn't hurt.

Once a month or so during the fall, Mom and I would drive to Des Moines, to visit a store called the Theatrical Shop. It was an amazing place, sort of like a mash-up between a Halloween store and a dance shop, all under the awning of an old movie theater. They had fabric, dance clothes, trim, wigs, theatrical makeup, props, shoes . . . everything. I used to love exploring the entire store. Then I'd get some new dance shorts and dance shoes, and pick out fabric for my next costume. We'd bring the fabric to

Marina and talk over what I wanted my costume to look like, and then Marina would sketch out the costume and make it for me. Not only did I get great costumes that fit perfectly, but it was also way cheaper, which was good because my family wasn't rich, and dancing cost a lot of money. So we did anything we could to hold down the costs.

I know I sound a little OCD, but it's the details that separate a good performance from a great one. When I'm up on that stage, the only person getting judged is me, so I need to make sure I'm happy with everything. If not, I have no one to blame but myself. Lots of people will tell you what to do, or what's good, or what's right. And I'm not saying you should ignore them—they are your mentors, coaches, family, and friends, and they're trying to help you. But at the end of the day, you've got to do what's right for you, no matter what anyone else says.

When I was eight years old, I entered a dance competition in Davenport, Iowa. I really wanted to win. It wasn't the biggest competition in the world, but Davenport was only fifty minutes away, so it was in my home territory. I had to go big. Michael Kohli and I spent months preparing my solo, which was a lyrical dance that we called "Ko Jun Dak."

Ko Jun Dak is how you would write my name in Chinese. In China, the family name ("Ko") comes first.

"Jun Dak" is my first name in Chinese. Ko means "tall," Jun means "smart," and Dak means "successful." I was hoping for at least two out of three to come true.

Lyrical dance has its roots in all kinds of styles: ballet, modern, jazz. It fuses all of them together, and it's beautiful. The pieces tend to be light, delicate, and very emotional, with lots of intricate footwork. Michael choreographed "Ko Jun Dak" to Bach's Prelude in C Major to highlight the fluidity of the lyrical style. Lyrical dance came naturally to me because of all the gymnastics I'd done.

To make "Ko Jun Dak" work, I needed a costume that looked both strong and graceful. The next time we visited the Theatrical Shop, I picked out a metallic gold fabric that would move like the scales on a dragon. Marina used it to make me a tank top with long fitted pants. Wearing them, I knew my routine would look amazing.

But not everyone agreed with me.

Immediately after I performed "Ko Jun Dak," one of the Applause judges signaled Michael over to the judges' table. That's never a good sign. I could tell Michael was getting annoyed, but I couldn't hear what she was saying. Then she started making big, angry gestures with her hands and called my mom over.

Uh-oh, I thought. This wasn't good. What did I do?

Could I have broken some rule? Forgotten my choreography? I tried to replay the performance in my head, but I couldn't figure out what had gone wrong. Instead, I sat there waiting nervously. Scores aren't announced until the end of the entire competition, and this was only day one, so I had a long wait ahead of me.

When Mom and Michael returned, they both tried to pretend everything was fine, but I could see their pursed lips and frowny foreheads. Something was definitely wrong.

"What's going on?" I asked.

"Nothing," Mom said. "You're fine. Perfect, as a matter of fact."

Michael nodded vigorously.

But if I hadn't done something wrong, why had they argued with the judge? No matter how much I asked, they wouldn't say anything. It wasn't until years later that Mom finally told me the truth.

The judge had given Michael a note. It read:

Be careful when you're costuming him. He's a boy, and I'm sure he's embarrassed to be seen in this.

Even now, it makes me angry.

I'm really glad Mom and Michael didn't show me that

note. It's hard enough being a male dancer around people not in the dance world. Other kids could be mean when they found out. The last thing I needed was for another dancer—an adult, even!—to make fun of me in the same way. And it was even worse because I was proud of my costume. Seeing that note would have crushed my confidence, which is the worst thing you can do to a young artist. Or to any kid, for that matter. If we don't believe in ourselves, how can we ever become the people we want to be?

For boys who want to be dancers or actors, this kind of thing is all too common. All I can say is this: it's happened to every male actor or dancer at some point in their lives, so we're in good company. Theater, dance—all the arts, really—they're about emotion, and there's a lot of people out there who think boys shouldn't show emotion, which sounds sad to me. I ignore them as much as I can.

Just to be clear: it's not easy for girls who want to make it as performers either. There will always be haters, and you've just got to prove them wrong.

I won First Place Overall at the competition, and when I accepted that trophy, I wasn't embarrassed about my outfit at all.

But even as I was winning trophies and coming into

myself as a person, something was on the horizon that would change everything. Soon, I wouldn't be dancing in competitions anymore. In fact, my whole world was about to change.

And not for the better.

The Diagnosis

Ever have one of those days when it feels like you wake up in the morning as yourself, but by the time you go to bed you're a completely different person? A day that throws everything into chaos, and leaves you scared to wonder what's going to happen next?

October 14, 2004, was that day for me.

If my life were a movie, there would have been a huge thunderstorm that morning, with a lot of lightning across the sky. Or I'd have woken up to some scary omen, like a big black crow sitting on my windowsill. Instead, the morning was cool, crisp, and sunny: a perfect fall day. I loved Iowa City on days like that. Dad and I would grab rakes and make piles of the beautiful multicolored leaves in the yard, or pedal our bikes out to the reservoir, or off to the university, or just aimlessly around the neighborhood enjoying the afternoon.

But not that day.

Matt was watching TV and I had spent most of the morning doing homework. Probably math. I loved math. It was neat and easy, and there was always a right answer. If only life were like that.

I knew something was wrong the moment Mom came home. It wasn't even dark out. Usually she didn't leave work until right before dinner. Her skin was pale and her eyes were red, as though she had been crying. She walked right up to her bedroom and closed the door behind her. *She must be sick*, I thought. So I wasn't surprised when Dad followed her upstairs. I kept doing my homework, and figured that he'd come down and tell me she had the flu or something. We'd probably make her some soup and watch one of her favorite movies after dinner. I was even kind of looking forward to it.

Little did I know . . .

It seemed like forever before Dad came back.

"Your mom needs to talk to you," he said. His voice was low and dull, like a robot with a busted battery.

My stomach clenched into one big knot. Even though I didn't know what was happening, I could tell it was bad. Dad usually joked around and made everyone laugh. He was always smiling. But not today, not now. He put his hand on my shoulder and squeezed gently.

Dad stayed back as Matt and I headed upstairs. My heart was pounding in my chest. I could tell Matt was scared too, because we walked really close to each other. We were so close, in fact, that I nearly knocked him down the steps at one point. Normally, he'd have headlocked me or called me clumsy, but he just steadied himself against the wall and kept walking. Neither of us said a thing.

When we got to her room, Mom was sitting on the bed with a balled-up wad of Kleenex in her hand. She patted the blanket next to her, and Matt and I climbed up. She looked at us for a while without saying anything. Finally, she let out a long, low breath.

"Everything is going to be okay," she said. "You understand? No matter what, everything is going to be okay."

She sniffed, and I could tell she was trying to be strong for Matt and me. Whatever she said next, I promised myself that I would be strong for her too.

"Your father has been diagnosed with liver cancer."

I froze.

Mom tried to keep talking, but her lip quivered and a sob broke through. She pushed her hand against her mouth, as though that would keep all the sadness from pouring out.

I had no idea what to do. I felt like I was stuck inside a big glass box, able to see everyone but unable to move. Mom's voice seemed to come from very far away, and there was a ringing in my ears, as though I'd stood too close to a loud noise. I couldn't make sense of the words she was saying. *Cancer? Dad?* That was impossible.

Mom said something about how they had caught it early, and that Dad was going to be fine, but Matt and I just stared at her with our mouths hanging open.

Your father has been diagnosed with liver cancer. Your father has been diagnosed with liver cancer. Your father has been diagnosed with liver cancer. Your father has been diagnosed with liver cancer. . . .

The words kept repeating in my mind on a loop going faster and faster.

Suddenly I realized Mom wasn't talking anymore. Instead, she was looking right at me, waiting for an answer.

"Sure," I said, even though I had no idea what she'd asked. Matt nodded too.

Mom smiled and wiped a hand across her forehead.

"I knew I could count on you boys," she said. She took a deep breath and blinked her eyes. When she opened them again, she was the energetic, no-nonsense Mom I knew.

"So!" she said, hopping off the bed. "It's decided. We'll

go out for sushi tonight. Now I have to pick up John. Will you boys be okay?"

I nodded, even though it no longer felt like a yes-or-no question. But Mom didn't seem to notice. She grabbed Matt and me in a tight hug.

"Everything's going to be all right," she whispered into my hair. "I love you."

Then she let us go.

Matt and I ran to our bedroom. I was shocked to see that the sun was still shining. Cars were driving by our window and people were going about their day, just like normal. But I felt as if years had passed in the last few minutes. I was older somehow: not in terms of days or months, but in experience. All of my life would now be divided up—before and after this moment.

Neither Matt nor I said a word. We were both lost in our own thoughts. I guess we're kind of typically midwestern in that way. My family doesn't make big displays of emotion. And we definitely don't dwell on things. When something bad happens, we absorb it and move on, always looking for the bright side and dealing with the dark.

But how were we supposed to move on from this? Dad had cancer. Nothing would ever be the same again.

CHAPTER 5

The Transplant

Of course, life went on as we continued with our normal routine. Mom was still working at ACT, and Dad still took care of us. We didn't talk much about his being sick. After that first big conversation with Mom, it became something we lived with but didn't focus on. My parents didn't hide it—I knew that it was serious enough that Dad had been put on a list for an emergency liver transplant—but since being sad couldn't fix anything, we just continued on as usual and hoped for the best. Every night I prayed for the cancer to go away. Every day I acted like nothing was wrong.

Maybe, more than anything else, this is what it takes to be a successful performer: you keep going. Hurt yourself in a rehearsal? Keep going. Lose a competition? Keep going. Get turned down for a part? Keep going. Someone you love gets sick? Keep. Going.

Dad's having cancer was, in a weird way, a lot like auditioning for a show. I was constantly hoping to hear news, good or bad.

Over the next few months, things changed gradually, so that it's hard for me to pinpoint exactly what happened when. Day by day, Dad had to take things more slowly. He started getting up later in the morning and going to bed earlier. He lost weight. The cancer was hard on his body. He had no energy and couldn't eat. He didn't lose his hair, but it became gray and thin. Some days he got up from bed just to sit on the couch until it was time to go to sleep again.

"I'm going to be fine," Dad said, whenever he caught me looking at him. "Alex, everything is going to be okay."

Then he'd grab a magazine and pretend to chase me around the house, like he had when I was little. But it was impossible to deny that he was sick, and that meant there were things he just couldn't do anymore.

"Boys, I need your help," I remember Mom telling us. "We all need to chip in around the house to keep things running."

Matt and I started doing more of the chores, the cooking and the cleaning. John did all that and took on the job of taking care of Matt and me—*and* continued working at Fareway grocery store to bring in money.

This was when the dance studio really became my second home. I was there nearly every day, sometimes until ten o'clock at night. It was my safe haven, the place where I could go to forget about Dad's cancer. In Michael's studio all I thought about was dance: the rhythm, the way my body flowed with the music, the single-minded drive to learn a step so that from the tips of my toes to the ends of my fingers it was perfect. Everything else in life was messy and complicated, but here, things could be perfect.

Dance was the happy place I went to, in order to drive all the other thoughts away. Just being physical made things seem better. Talk to any athlete, and we'll tell you the same thing. If we're sad, or upset, or just feel like we're completely stuck and can't see a way forward—we get up and move. It won't change the world, but it might change the way we feel about things. And once we feel different, we can change our world.

But even at the studio there were problems.

"We have to save more money," I remember Mom telling John and me one day. "We're going to have a lot of medical bills."

Mom had great insurance through the ACT, but even with a good job, it was hard to raise three boys, pay for

Dad's treatment, and keep a roof over our heads. Much as I loved them, it became harder and harder to justify paying for dance lessons. And it wasn't just the lessons: there were the costumes, the travel costs, the competition expenses. It all added up.

Thankfully, Mom had a brilliant idea.

One day after rehearsal, she asked Michael if they could talk. Michael was very close to our family, and she could tell something had been wrong for a while.

"Sam is sick," Mom told Michael. "He has cancer."

"Oh, Tammie," Michael said, putting her hand on Mom's arm. "I'm so sorry."

"Thank you," Mom replied, nodding slightly. She squared her shoulders and took a deep breath. I knew what she was about to do was hard for her, and I knew she was doing it for me. I took her hand in mine and squeezed it.

"Money is a little tight right now," Mom continued. "Is there any way I can help out around the studio so the boys can continue taking classes?"

"Of course!" Michael responded instantly. "You know I love having them here. Don't worry—we'll make this work."

Soon it was settled. Mom would help Michael with her computers, her spreadsheets, and the costumes. In exchange, we would get a full scholarship for our classes.

This was good because Dad's cancer was worsening fast. I didn't know a lot about liver cancer before Dad was diagnosed, but I soon found out that it's a pretty bad kind. Only 14 percent of people survive more than five years after being diagnosed. The best chance of surviving is to have a full liver transplant, but that means finding a compatible donor, which can take a while. A liver isn't like a kidney, which people have two of. Everyone has one liver, and they need the whole thing, so we were waiting for someone with a healthy, compatible liver to pass on. It made me realize how important it is to be an organ donor. Donors *literally* save lives. As soon as I'm old enough, I'm going to register to become an organ donor. I know it's what Dad would have wanted.

I became totally focused on Dad getting a liver transplant. I thought that as soon as he had a new liver, he would be fixed—like when you put a new battery in a remote control. I know that's naive, but I wanted to believe there was an easy solution to all our problems. So when the call came in early January telling us there was a liver waiting for Dad at the hospital, I was overjoyed. *Finally*, I thought, our lives would go back to normal.

I was so wrong.

Liver transplant surgery is really delicate. One inch in

the wrong direction, and who knows what they'd be cutting through? They told us that Dad's transplant could easily take twelve hours, so we packed up everything we thought we might possibly want: games, movies, books, snacks, you name it. We even had a portable TV. We were ready for the long haul.

When we got to the hospital, they rushed Dad off to get ready for his surgery. Mom, Matt, John, and I settled into the waiting room, where we waited . . . and waited. Twelve hours went by before someone came to see us.

"I'm very sorry to tell you this," said Dr. Katz, our surgeon. "But Sam isn't going to have a transplant today."

We were so confused, I felt like crying. No one told us this beforehand, but here's how liver transplants work: After you're diagnosed, your name goes on a list. Everyone on the list is checked and double-checked to make sure they're healthy enough to survive the transplant. Unlike with other organs, it doesn't matter how long you've been waiting—the only thing that matters is how much you need the liver, and how likely you are to survive the surgery. In a way, Dad was lucky, because he was pretty healthy (other than his liver), and he desperately needed the transplant. So he shot right to the top of the list. That's why it was only a few months after his diagnosis that he got called in for surgery.

But there are so few healthy livers available that anytime someone is up for a transplant, the doctors always bring in a backup recipient, in case something goes wrong or the first person fails their final physical. If they didn't have a backup person prepped and ready for surgery, the donor liver might not still be viable by the time they find someone else. They don't tell you that you're the backup, because they're worried you might not take it seriously if they did.

This time, Dad was the backup. I was crushed, but I tried not to let it show because I knew it was worse for him. When they wheeled him back to us, he was quieter than I'd ever seen him, as though his mind were far away.

"Soon," Dr. Katz told us. "You're at the top of the list now."

Twelve days later, the hospital called again. This time, Dr. Katz assured us, it was the real deal. So we repacked our portable TV and headed back to the university.

"Good luck," I told Dad as they prepared to wheel him away. He held my hand gently.

"I don't need luck," he said. "Remember, everything is going to be okay. I'll see you when I'm done."

Outside the hospital windows, it was gray and chilly. January in Iowa can be viciously cold. But inside, I'd never felt so warm.

"This is your father's best shot for beating the cancer," Dr. Katz had explained. As we sat in the waiting room, with its bright fluorescent lights and soft-carpeted floors, I imagined what it would be like to wake up tomorrow and know my father was better. It sounded like a dream come true.

But as the hours passed with no word from the doctors, I grew more and more worried. What if something had gone wrong? We hunkered down in the waiting room like a city under siege. I tried to play a game, or read a book, but I couldn't concentrate on anything. It grew dark outside, and the wind moaned against the bare trees. All the bad omens I'd looked for on the day of Dad's diagnosis were here now. I just hoped they didn't mean anything this time.

Matt and I napped and ate and did our homework. Sometimes we talked, but it was hard to keep a conversation going when we all knew what was happening in the operating room. Just about the only thing I could pay attention to was *The Princess Diaries*, one of the few movies we'd brought with us. It was just the right amount of mindless fun. Matt and I must have watched it three or four times that day.

Finally, after ten hours, Mom couldn't take it anymore.

Before I was born, she had interned at the hospital during her PhD program, and she still knew people in the administration. After a bunch of frantic calls and a whole lot of waiting, she got some answers.

"They're having trouble with the incisions they need to make to do the surgery," an administrator told her. "And there have been some *minor* complications."

"What do you mean?" Mom asked.

"The donor liver is unexpectedly large, but everything's all right," the administrator hurried to assure us. "Dr. Katz has him open on the surgical table, and he's working on it."

My heart nearly stopped. I couldn't believe what they were saying. My dad—my happy, loving dad—was on a table somewhere, cut open, empty. Unless they got the new liver in fast, they'd have to put his old one back in, which meant the cancer would have more time to spread. Every day he spent with his old liver inside him brought him closer to death. If I could have given him mine, I would have.

Mom continued talking on the phone, and we found out it was even worse than we had imagined. Dad had an old scar on his abdomen, from a previous surgery, and it was right where they needed to make the incision for the transplant. But scar tissue is tough, and it made the entire surgery that much more difficult (and painful, and harder to recover from).

"He'll be in the O.R. for at least a few more hours," the administrator finished. "At least."

In the end, Dad was in surgery for eighteen hours. But it was a success. The liver ended up fitting, though just barely. Because of the scar tissue, Dr. Katz had to cut Dad up and restitch and restaple him numerous times. The IV that gave him blood transfusions through the arteries in his neck kept collapsing, and they had to redo it over and over again. By the time they were done, he was like a pincushion—and he'd received nearly six liters of blood. That's as much as the average adult male has in his entire body. In recovery, he looked almost Frankenstein-ish. We nicknamed him "Liver Bumpy," because you could literally see where the big new liver protruded from Dad's otherwise skinny frame.

To this day, I don't know where that liver came from. I don't know the name of the person who gave it to us, or what their life was like, or who they left behind. I don't even know if it was a man or a woman. But I will be in their debt forever. Thank you, whoever you are. Thank you. You didn't just give a profound gift to my dad, you gave a gift to our entire family.

Even once the surgery was over, it was a long time

before our family returned to normal. In fact, now that I think about it, we never really did. The next two years would bring one big change after another. My life wouldn't have any real "normal" or sense of routine until I found myself on Broadway, which is about the most abnormal normal I can imagine.

But Dad had a long road ahead of him, and I would be alongside him the entire way.

The Ride

"Are you sure you're ready for this?" Mom asked as she watched Matt, John, Dad, and me buckle our helmets on. She couldn't hide the worry in her voice. "I mean, it just seems awfully soon."

"I'm fine, Tammie, I promise," Dad said as he dropped a water bottle into his backpack. It was a little after nine a.m., the sun was shining brightly in a perfect July sky, and we had an awesome day planned.

It was a little over a year after Dad's surgery. His recovery from the transplant had been difficult. For the first week, his condition was so touch and go that he couldn't leave the intensive care unit. After that, he had another week in a regular recovery room before he could actually come home, and even then, he still wasn't very strong. His body had been cut open and torn apart. He almost seemed sicker than he had before the transplant, because he was so fragile. The first time he left the house for a walk, my mom had to support him the entire way—and they only went to the stop sign at the end of the block. But week by week he got stronger.

Immediately after his surgery, a steady stream of relatives came to stay with us and help out. For weeks at a time, my aunties Alicia, Kitty, and Kristin lived in our spare bedroom and did everything from grocery shopping to taking Dad to his doctor's appointments. And they weren't the only ones. Our neighbors came by with plates of food and offers to help with yard work and cleaning. Dr. Katz had become a good friend of the family, and he often came by to check on us, as did our neighbors, Joe and Shirley Abdo. Dmitri and Marina Trouch, Michael Kohli, and all the other people we'd met through dance and gymnastics were always eager to lend a hand. Without all of their support, I don't know what we would have done. My mom was nearly exhausted from the effort of working and keeping our house together, but with the help of friends and extended family, we were able to get back on our feet.

Weeks turned to months. My aunties went home. Dad continued to recover. The doctors recommended he come in for a physical every half year, to make sure the cancer hadn't returned. When he passed his first checkup with flying colors, it was like we had all been holding our breath without realizing it. Suddenly a weight left our shoulders. When Dad passed the second physical with no problems, we thought we were in the clear. A year cancer-free! To celebrate, we decided to go on a very special bike ride: the *Register*'s Annual Great Bicycle Ride Across Iowa, or RAGBRAI.

In Iowa, RAGBRAI is a big deal. It began in the early seventies and has been held every year since. Each summer, thousands of cyclists get together to ride from one end of the state to the other. It's not a race—there's no winning—it's just a great ride through lots of cool small towns and beautiful open fields. It's broken up into multiple sections, done over the course of a week. Every year the route is adjusted to go through different communities in Iowa. We'd never done it before, but we always talked about it, and this year, the ride was going right by Iowa City. Now, with Dad out of the hospital, it seemed like the perfect year to take part.

And there was another reason: Lance Armstrong was doing the ride for the first time ever! Not only did he survive having cancer in his testicles, lungs, and brain, but immediately after he recovered, he won the Tour de France bike race—seven times in a row. When we heard that he was at RAGBRAI to raise awareness for his cancer work with Team Livestrong, the ride seemed like something we just had to do—even if it made Mom nervous.

"Okaaaay," she said as we stood in the driveway waiting to kick off. "You boys be careful."

In this case, I was pretty sure we "boys" included my father.

"Of course!" we said in unison. Soon we were pedaling down Teg Drive and off to the ride.

I couldn't have imagined a more perfect day for cycling. The sky was clear and bright. I slipped into an easy rhythm, pedaling slow and steady. When we hit the first little hill on our way out of the neighborhood, I stood up on my pedals and coasted into the wind, my eyes closed, the sun warming my face. It felt like riding into pure joy.

We were meeting up with RAGBRAI on day two of the ride, in a town called Coralville, which was about twenty-five minutes by bike from where we lived. We'd heard that Lance was going to give a speech, and we didn't want to miss out on it.

In fact, since Dad's transplant, we'd been doing a lot of things to make sure we didn't miss out on them. Being that close to death had given Dad an awareness of how short life could be. From now on, he said, he wasn't missing out on anything, so that's how we lived. Because he loved good food, we went out to eat more often. Mom wanted to find a way for us to go to Nepal, because my father had always dreamed of seeing Mount Everest, but the doctors said it wasn't safe. Instead, we started planning a trip to California, for Dad to see his mom, who we called Po Po.

I learned an important lesson that year: it's easy to miss out on great things because they require extra effort, and we think we have all the time in the world to do them "later." But nothing is guaranteed. Take advantage of now, because you don't know what tomorrow will bring. RAGBRAI and Lance Armstrong's speech were two things Dad wanted to take advantage of while we could.

On our way to RAGBRAI, we rode in a neat little line: first Dad, then me, then Matt, then John, each on a different-colored bike. I'd had mine forever. It was a little red Trek bike that I'd gotten from Walmart for seventy dollars. It wasn't fancy, but it fit me well and I'd been riding it for years. Dad had a silver Raleigh, John had a red one, and Matt had a nearly new blue Trek bike. Together, we were just a shade off from being the colors of the American flag!

Along the way, we passed lots of other cyclists. Iowa City is a bike-friendly place, and around RAGBRAI, you couldn't go more than a block without seeing someone riding. Everyone knew where we were headed, and people on the streets smiled and waved or honked their horns as we passed. I knew it wasn't personal, but I still felt like they were talking especially to us. "Congratulations," I imagined they were saying, "You did it! You beat cancer!"

When we finally reached the official rally point, it was like a giant street fair. There were blocks and blocks of food stalls, games, and street vendors selling souvenirs. We locked our bikes to a lamppost and wandered through the crowd.

"How are you doing?" I asked Dad. The ride had been his idea, but I couldn't help but worry. Even though there were no signs that his cancer had returned, he still had bad days when he had no energy and everything hurt. If getting there had been too hard for him, I figured we could enjoy the festival and skip the ride. The important part wasn't what we did, it was that we did it together.

"I don't feel good," Dad replied.

My heart started pounding. If I called Mom now, I wondered how soon she could pick us up. *Or maybe we should just find an ambulance*, I thought. I scanned the crowd for an emergency first-aid station.

Then Dad laughed.

"I don't feel good," he repeated. "I feel great! It's a beautiful day, I've got my boys with me, and we're going to hear Lance Armstrong speak. And I can't wait to get back on my bike!" He put one arm on my shoulder and the other around Matt. Together, the four of us made our way to the stage where Lance was being introduced.

I was so excited I could barely contain myself.

In fact, I was so thrilled to hear Lance talk that I didn't listen to a word he said. I spent the whole time thrilled. *Wow! That's really Lance Armstrong!* Then, the next thing I knew, he was getting off the stage. I'd been there for the entire speech, and yet somehow I managed to miss the whole thing. I know he talked about cancer research, and raising money, and making a difference, but if you asked me now, I probably couldn't tell you a single specific thing he said.

Oh well, I thought to myself. *At least I can say that I heard him. That means something!*

I was a little bummed out, but I didn't let it show—mostly because I didn't want Dad to know that I'd daydreamed through the whole talk. As Lance stepped offstage, the four of us began to worm our way out of the crowd and back to where we'd left our bikes. But it was impossible to get anywhere. There were thousands of people, some milling around the booths, others trying to get on their bikes and head to the starting place. We managed to move about three feet in ten minutes.

"Excuse me," Dad said. "Sorry! Coming through."

People tried to get out of the way, but there wasn't anywhere for them to go. The crowd pushed us this way and that. I stumbled over someone's foot and looked up to apologize.

"I'm sorry," I said to the tall man before me wearing bright yellow. He looked down at me and smiled, and that's when I realized:

I'd just stepped on Lance Armstrong!

"Hey man," he said. "It's cool."

"You're—I—you!" I was so excited, I couldn't speak.

"I'm Lance," he said. "Lance Armstrong. You guys riding today?"

He gestured at John, Matt, Dad, and me. We all nodded furiously.

"I'm Alex," I introduced myself, and so did Matt, John, and Dad.

"Alex, John, Matt, Sam," Lance repeated. I felt a chill run up my spine. Lance Armstrong knew my name! "Good luck." He smiled. "I'll see you out on the route!"

He shook each of our hands and then turned back to his friends. The crowd shifted again, and as suddenly as he had appeared next to us, he was gone. I couldn't believe it. I'd actually spoken to Lance Armstrong! It was a dream come true.

"Wow!" Matt said. "We should have gotten his autograph."

"Next year." Dad smiled. "We'll be back. Now let's grab our bikes and get pedaling!"

We only rode ten miles or so with the crowd—just enough to say that we had done it. Even though we were our own little slow-going bubble, we were within the larger river of RAGBRAI. It was like a parade with no floats, or a party on wheels. Everyone was laughing: me, John, Matt, Dad, and a thousand smiling strangers who were all happy to see us. We jockeyed for position playfully, each of us passing the others and then slowing down, like we were leapfrogging our way through the race. It was one of the best bike rides of my life.

Next year, I promised myself, *we'll do the whole thing.*

But it didn't work out that way.

On that perfect July afternoon, I felt like I could see forever. The road stretched out before me: gentle and smooth, filled with family and new friends. I wanted life to always be like this, but of course nothing ever stays the same. Even though I could see all the way to the horizon, I couldn't see what was coming.

Dad's cancer was returning.

Six months from now he would start to feel tired and achy again. In nine months, the doctors would confirm that his cancer was back, and it was worse this time. It had spread beyond his liver to his entire vascular system. It was in his lymph nodes and his blood vessels. There would be no second transplant. Once he was diagnosed, he was already too sick to get on the list. In fact, he was too sick for most treatments. His body, which seemed so strong as we pedaled our way through Iowa City on that July day, would give out all at once. By the time RAGBRAI came around next year, Dad was dead.

My family had a perfect summer, and we cherished every moment of it. Somehow, it seemed like both the longest and shortest summer of my life. In my memory, every day was sunny and warm. We did more than ever, but it ended far too soon. The days flew past us like birds in a flock: one moment you can see hundreds of them coming toward you, and the next just a few stragglers, struggling to escape the cold winds of winter.

But amid all the terrible things that were headed our way, something amazing happened—something I had wanted my entire life but thought would never occur. In the two brief months between my father's second diagnosis and his passing, he gave me the greatest gift any child can receive from a parent: his blessing.

The Conversation

Dad had to be admitted to the emergency room just a week after we found out his cancer had returned. His body was shutting down, and he was too sick to be at home. From then on, he was in and out of the hospital virtually every few days. Mom took time off from work, and when it became clear things weren't improving, she traded in her regular job with the ACT for a part-time teaching position. Money was tight, but time with Dad was more important. We visited him as often as we could, although there were many days when he was too sick to see us, or he slept through visiting hours. He was on a lot of pain medication, and most of the time when I saw him, we couldn't really talk. I would hold his hand and sit next to him, or tell him about my day, or help bring a small glass of water to his lips, which were always dry. Mostly we would watch the news or read. But one afternoon, he told Mom that he needed to talk to me—just me, alone.

"Remember, he needs his rest," Mom said as we stood by the door to his room. "If he looks tired, let him sleep. You okay to do this on your own?"

I nodded. Dad being sick had given me a terrible fear of hospitals. I hated the way they smelled, a mixture of sick and sterile, soap and medicine. I hated all the sounds: the beeping machines, the whispering doctors, the crying patients. But most of all, I hated thinking about my dad being trapped here by himself, not knowing when or if he'd be able to come home and see his family again.

"I love you," Mom said, and kissed me on the forehead. "Be strong, for him."

I opened the door.

In the big metal hospital bed, Dad looked small—smaller than I had ever seen him. It wasn't just the weight he'd lost. It was as though the cancer had shrunk him somehow, or taken something from him. Or maybe it was just that he was surrounded by giant machines that monitored his heart, kept him hydrated, and pumped fluids into and out of his body. Next to all that metal, how could a person look anything but small?

"Mom said you wanted to talk?" I whispered. Dad's eyes were closed and his chest was rising and falling softly.

As I stood in the doorway, I wondered if he was asleep. If so, I didn't want to wake him. After everything he'd been through, he needed rest. And it was nice, for once, to see the lines of worry and fear gone from his face. In sleep, he looked like the Dad I knew.

"Alex?" he mumbled. His left eye peeked open. He squinted at me and rubbed his face. "Come in, come in."

He sounded exhausted, as if even talking took too much effort. He was sicker now than he'd ever been, and we knew he didn't have much time left.

"Help me with this," he said, gesturing to a big piece of plastic connected to his bed by a chunky beige cord. "But watch out for the red button—that calls the nurse."

I helped him use the remote to raise his bed so that he was sitting upright. Even that tiny bit of work made beads of sweat appear on his face. With a lot of effort, he scooted over to make room on the bed and gestured for me to sit next to him.

I clambered up onto the mattress, carefully avoiding all the medical equipment. I knew the machines were there to keep Dad healthy, but I couldn't help but associate them with his sickness. I tried as hard as I could to pretend they didn't exist.

"We need to talk," Dad said. "And I want you to listen very carefully, because this is important. I know the last few weeks have been hard, but can you do that?"

I nodded. My heart fluttered in my chest. I wanted to be anywhere but here. I couldn't imagine what he was going to tell me, though I was pretty sure I didn't want to hear it. But whatever he had to say, I told myself that I would be strong. We would get through this, like we did everything, as a family.

"I want to talk about your future," Dad said. He grimaced as a wave of pain coursed through him.

Oh, no, I thought. *Here it comes.* We were in a hospital—of course Dad wanted to talk about my future. He probably wanted to introduce me to his doctors so I could see what an awesome job they had. I felt bad, honestly: if I had never discovered dance, I think I would have become a doctor of some kind, and I know Dad would have loved that—though I also knew that he would love me no matter what I did. But you can love someone and still think they're making the wrong choices.

But if he was feeling well enough to tell me what I should do with my life, then maybe—just maybe—there was a chance he might still recover. I settled into my seat, prepared to hear all about how my hands were "perfectly shaped" for a surgeon.

"Your mom and I aren't going to be around forever," Dad began.

"Did—" I started, but Dad held up his hand to stop me.

"I'm sick, Alex," Dad said. My heart began to pound. He and I never talked about serious things like this. "Very, very sick. But even if the cancer went away tomorrow, none of us stays on this earth forever. There will come a day, hopefully many, many years from now, when your mom and I won't be here to look after you and your brothers. I need to know that you're going to be able to take care of yourself."

And this is it, I thought. Next he'd tell me that dancing wasn't a secure career, and I needed to find something dependable. *And maybe he's right,* I thought. Maybe I was just setting myself up for a life of struggle and heartbreak. But it was *my* life, and dancing was the thing I wanted to do with it.

"Dancing . . ." Dad paused. I stared down at the bed because I knew what was coming, and it made me sad. I didn't want to argue with him, and I knew he had my best interests at heart. But couldn't he see that dancing was all I ever wanted to do? That dancing was the thing I felt *called* to do? I couldn't look him in the eye and listen to him say it was wrong when it felt so right.

Dad's big warm hand cupped the back of my head, lifting my face up to look at him. He was smiling—a genuine, giant Dad smile, the kind I hadn't seen on him since the cancer returned. I couldn't help but smile back.

"Dancing is the thing that matters most to you in the whole world, isn't it?"

It was as though the entire room had gone still. All I could hear was the hushed whirring of the machines around us. Even my heart seemed to be holding its breath.

"Yes," I whispered.

"Then that's what you're supposed to do. I believe God gave you a great gift, and you're going to use it to become the best dancer in the world. Do you hear me? The best."

I was so shocked, I couldn't think. I wouldn't have been more surprised if Dad had told me he was going to become a dancer himself.

"Dad, do you . . . really? I—"

I wanted to say thank you, and that I loved him, and that I had never felt so happy in my whole life, but all the words got tangled around one another and I couldn't get them out.

As I fumbled, Dad started laughing. It was a small, careful laugh at first—the kind you hear in hospitals, where people are afraid of waking someone up, or hurting themselves. But soon it grew, and I couldn't help but join in. The next thing I knew the two of us were laughing tremendous big belly laughs.

"Stop, stop!" Dad said, half gasping for breath. "I'm a sick man, you know!"

But that just made me laugh harder, like I was laughing out all the stress and tension of the last week in one great big burst. I felt light, like I weighed nothing. I wanted to get up and dance right then and there!

When Dad finally got his breath back, he held up his hand to get my attention again.

"But," he began, and I froze. *But what?* I wondered.

"But you need to make some changes," he continued. He looked at me seriously, and I could feel something shift between us. It was as though we were talking adult to adult. I was still his son, but I was also my own person, and Dad was talking to both versions of me at the same time. I needed to be more of a grown-up now—for him, for Mom, for Matt and John, and most importantly, for myself.

"This dancing that you've been doing—the competitions, the classes, the jumping around—it needs to stop. I don't say this to hurt you, but it's not serious."

Not serious? Now I was confused.

"The basis for all dance—all serious dance—is ballet," Dad continued. "If you are going to be a real dancer, a *professional* dancer, you have to put all this other . . . *aerobics* aside. From now on, you will study ballet, and you will become the best ballet dancer, like Baryshnikov, because you have it in you."

"Ballet?" I said. I'd only ever taken a few lessons in ballet. I liked it, but . . .

"Ballet," Dad said firmly. "Everything comes from ballet. And we need to find you a new studio. You need to study with the best, because you will be the best. Remember that," he said, and pointed at my head. "If you want to be the best, you must always study from the best."

Something wet splashed against my hand, and I realized I was crying. I felt like Dad had seen me—the real me—for the first time. I couldn't stop myself from grabbing him and hugging him tightly.

"Be careful," he whispered.

"Thank you, Dad," I said, tears running down my face. "And I promise, just you wait. I'm going to be the best ballet dancer you've ever seen."

I just hoped that he lived to see me. *Please God*, I prayed, *let us keep him long enough that I can perform for him. Let me make him proud.*

"I know it, Alex," Dad said. "I love you."

"I love you too, Dad."

We sat there in silence for a moment, before the

nurse came and I had to leave. My mind was spinning, but I felt . . . *right*. Suddenly there was a certainty in my heart that I was on the path God intended for me.

But I had no way of knowing all the strange, awful, and awesome places it was going to lead me over the next few years. . . .

A Beginning, and an End

Dad stayed in the hospital for a while that time, and when he came back, he was a different person. He was still my funny, loving dad, but now the cancer had gotten ahold of him, and it never let go again. He got skinnier and skinnier. When he was awake, he spent most of his time on the couch talking to our minister, Pastor Lee. They spent hours together every week. Sometimes I stayed and prayed with them, but more often I sat in my room with the door open so their conversations would drift in. I wanted to hear their voices, but not the words: no death, or heaven, or sickness, just the comforting sounds of two of the most important men in my life talking. Sometimes, I could almost forget what they were talking about. But it always came rushing back eventually.

I was itching to intensify my study of ballet. I wanted to show Dad that I'd taken what he said to heart, and I knew time was short. Michael offered ballet and technique classes, but her studio focused on competition and jazz dancing. If I wanted to be the best dancer I could be, I needed teachers who specialized in ballet. After all, I wouldn't expect a math teacher—even a brilliant, talented genius of a math teacher—to help me with my writing. In dance, it's the same way. It isn't enough to have a *good* dance teacher. You need a good dance teacher who concentrates on the right kind of dance.

Leaving Michael's studio was hard. She was almost family, in a way, especially after Dad got sick. I think she was a little hurt that I needed to move on, but she understood. If I could have continued doing dancing with her while learning ballet, I would have. But ballet isn't like that. It requires all of your attention, all of your time. It is the most difficult and rewarding kind of dance there is. My father was right: God had given me a gift, and I needed to live up to that responsibility.

There were basically two big dance studios in Iowa City: the National Dance Academy (where I studied with Michael) and the Nolte Academy of Dance. Nolte wasn't as grand as National Dance Academy back then. But it was starting to be known for its rigorous ballet training. The school had recently brought in a prestigious new teacher named Tad Snider. It seemed like fate that he would appear right when I needed him—yet another sign that this was the path I was meant to be on.

"This is especially good," Mom said as we toured the studio, "because you need a male mentor."

Up until now, I'd had only female dance instructors. They were fantastic, and the dance education I'd received was top-notch. But in ballet, men and women have very distinct roles, and they come with different skills that you need to master. If I was going to be an elite ballet dancer, I needed male teachers in my life. Tad seemed like a godsend.

From the beginning, Tad singled me out for special attention. I'd been training for only a few weeks, and I'd already been cast in Nolte's production of *The Nutcracker.* I was sitting on the sidelines during rehearsal one day, stretching. Ballet, more than any other kind of dance, requires that your body be able to assume certain positions. Your feet have to be able to point, your hips have to be able to turn out. If you can't mold your body into the right shape, then your first, last, and constant job is to stretch until you can. Sitting, standing—even sleeping—you should be stretching.

"Hey Alex," Tad said, squatting next to me as I tried to arch my foot farther than it wanted to go. "Do you know how to do a *tour*?"

"No," I said, shaking my head. To be honest, I wasn't even certain what a *tour* was, or why I needed to know it.

Tad nodded, making a mental note. He was a serious teacher. Occasionally he joked around, but he was very focused on the work. Perhaps because he looked so young, he needed to be more serious in order to get people to listen. With his big eyes and floppy brown hair, he could easily have been a teenager visiting his younger brother at our rehearsal.

"I'm going to teach you," he said. "Come on."

He gestured over to a quiet corner of the rehearsal room. As I walked, I watched my reflection in the big front mirror. A dozen girls in tights and ballet slippers were lined up against the barre, practicing. Nolte was a small school, so there were only about twenty of us in the room.

"Sit," Tad said, pushing his hands together in front of him and gesturing at the ground. He stood straight and peered up toward the ceiling, in his teaching pose. "Let's see, how to explain a *tour*? The word's actually French and is short for *tour en l'air*, which literally means 'turn in the air.' It's one of the basic jumps that all male ballet dancers must master. Jumps and lifts are the two most important skills guys have in ballet. Now watch!"

Suddenly Tad leaped into the air. His body was fully extended down through his toes, like a human pencil. As he reached the peak of his jump, he seemed to float in graceful slowness *and* spin in a lightning-fast full rotation at the same time. He landed, but he stayed on the ground for only a split second before he jumped again. This time, he spun around twice.

"That's a double *tour*. Some dancers, like Nijinsky, could even do triples." He paused, a rare smile lighting up his face. "But we'll start you with the basics and work our way up. To begin, assume fifth position."

In ballet, there are five basic alignments for your feet, with corresponding positions for the hands—first through fifth position. Fifth position is when your feet are parallel, one in front of the other, toes pointing in opposite directions so that the heel of one foot touches the toes of the other—if you can stretch that far. It took me a while.

After I got in position, Tad explained that in order to do a *tour*, I needed to jump, point my feet while I was in the air, do one full rotation, and land back in fifth position.

"Make sure you spot before you jump," he said. "You know that, right?"

I nodded. Gymnastics had given me a leg up in ballet. Because of all the tumbling I'd been doing, I knew a lot about jumping, spinning, and keeping my balance. One of the big tricks is to spot before you turn. *Spotting* means staring at a point on the wall that you want to end up facing. When you spin, you move your head as swiftly as possible, so that you only take your eyes off your spot for the briefest moment. Your head should rotate much faster than the rest of your body. This keeps you from getting dizzy.

For the rest of rehearsal, Tad had me assume fifth position, spot, jump, and land, without any rotation. We never did any full *tours* that day, but from then on, whenever we had a free moment, Tad drilled me. Until I had those parts perfect, he didn't even want me to try the rotation. Instead, we built the skill up slowly, piece by piece. It took weeks for me to learn how to do perfect *tours*. Those little tips from Tad evolved into private lessons, and soon I was studying with him almost constantly.

I'd been pretty dedicated to dance before this, but now I was at a whole different level. I had my father's blessing, which had been the last thing holding me back. And I had only a short time to prove that I was taking ballet seriously. So I studied constantly, wanting to show Dad what I was capable of.

But it wasn't enough. I needed years of training before I'd be a great ballet dancer, and my father didn't have years. He had months, maybe weeks—maybe days. I felt like an invisible timer was hovering over my head. I could hear it ticking, but I had no way of knowing when it would hit zero.

Travels with My Dad

As the plane circled Chicago's O'Hare airport, Dad began to feel weak. The color drained from his face, and even though sweat was dripping down his forehead, he shivered.

"Excuse me, but could we get a blanket, please?" Mom asked the flight attendant. We were flying coach, and it looked like she was about to tell us they didn't have blankets on board. But then she saw Dad.

"Of course. I'll find something," she said.

When she came back, she brought him a blanket and gently tucked it in around him. Even though she didn't know about the cancer, it was obvious by this point that Dad was dying, and everyone could see it.

By the time we landed, Dad needed a wheelchair to make our connecting flight. It made me wonder if this trip had been a good idea. Dad desperately wanted to see his mother before he died, but she had Alzheimer's and was too sick to leave California. So we were going to her.

Everyone knew this would be the last trip, so our entire extended family was gathering for a week in San Jose. My cousins Emily and Pearl drove from San Francisco, my auntie Alicia and uncle Franco flew in from Las Vegas, and my auntie Kristin, uncle David, and their kids, Ashleigh and Alissa, flew up from Los Angeles. Other relatives also came from all over California. But Po Po was too sick to leave Oakland, so we had to go visit her. Because she had Alzheimer's, no one had told her that Dad had cancer.

As we arrived in San Jose, Mom kept checking to make sure Dad felt okay. Maybe it was the ocean breeze, or knowing that he would soon see his mother, but as soon as he stepped off the plane in California, a twinkle returned to Dad's eye. For the first time in a while, it was like he wasn't sick. When the flight attendants asked if he needed a wheelchair, he waved them away. He held Mom's arm, but he walked out of the airport on his own two feet, and I could tell how happy that made him.

We rented a giant minivan so that we could do touristy things but always have a place where Dad could sit (or even lie down) if he needed.

"Your dad is very sick," Mom had cautioned us before we left, "so we might not do a lot of activities. Okay? We're going to only do what Dad can do, and that'll have to be enough."

"Always looking out for me." Dad smiled and kissed her on the cheek. I knew it made him sad to admit how sick he was, but he was happy to have such a wife, who cared for him so much.

Luckily, Dad found a reserve of strength somewhere deep inside him. For that entire week in California, it was as though he wasn't sick. We went everywhere. It was the best trip of my life.

One of my favorite parts was dinner at Auntie Polly's house. It was like footage from a Disney movie. Everyone was just so happy. Auntie Polly made dinner for about one hundred when there were only about fifteen of us. Every single dish was a different color and had a different taste. There was so much laughter and joy in the room, I never wanted to go. Leaving her house was like the day after Christmas. You couldn't wait until the next time.

My favorite memory was being at the ocean with my dad. Dad loved the ocean, so we spent at least part of every day by the water. He took Matt and me to see the seals on the pier at Santa Cruz. We went to Monterey Bay to watch the surfers, and to visit the aquarium. In the afternoon, we played games on the boardwalk with our cousins, who we never got to see much. Dad watched with a smile on his face. He was always happiest when we were all together.

"Family," Uncle David said as he dropped down to sit next to my father. "It's the most important thing in life. We should do this more often."

He was talking to Dad, but he looked at me as he said it. I knew "we" would never do this again, but it reminded me that family didn't just mean my parents and brothers. I had a great big extended family, and even if we didn't see each other often, we still loved each other very much. I knew Uncle David was right: family was the most important thing. When Dad was gone, we would be the ones to remember for each other, to comfort each other, and to tell the stories of Dad's life that would make us laugh and cry for decades to come. But for now, I was happy just to be in the same place as them, feeling the same sun shining on all our smiling faces, even Dad's. I stared out at the ocean, and wished his life would go on forever, just like the sparkling water in front of me. But I knew it wouldn't.

We visited Oakland to see Po Po, who I'd only known when I was a baby. She was like a little-old-lady version of Dad, always sweet and smiling. We went all around

Chinatown, where she lived, seeing the sights. Everyone seemed to know her, even if often she couldn't remember them. But it was clear that she was well loved, and seeing how happy she was—even though she was sick—made Dad even happier.

"This is very much like Hong Kong," Dad told me as we wandered past bright red-and-gold awnings above stalls selling vegetables and live crabs in buckets. I slipped my hand into Dad's, and for a moment I imagined we were in Hong Kong together. I knew we'd never make it there, but at least we had right now, and I could pretend.

"There's someone else we need to see," Dad said one afternoon, after we'd left Po Po to take a nap. The whole family got in the minivan and drove out beyond the city limits.

"Where are we going?" I asked.

"You'll see" was all he would say.

When we pulled up at the cemetery, I understood. It took a while to get to the grave, because Dad had grown tired from walking around all day, but finally we stopped in front of a small tombstone in a large, grassy field.

"This is where my father is buried," Dad said. He placed a colorful bouquet of flowers in front of the stone, which was dark, weathered granite. Then he looked at the clear space next to it. "And this is where *your* father will be buried."

He put his arm around my shoulder. I looked at the innocent patch of grass. It was so fresh, green, and beautiful. It seemed impossible to believe that one day, Dad would be buried beneath it. A chill ran down my spine. I didn't want to be here. I didn't want to think about this. The entire trip had been so normal. No one had cried, not since we'd arrived in San Jose, and Dad had been strong again. But there was no escaping the future.

We stood silently, side by side, looking at the graves of our fathers. For the first time in my life, I began to understand what it felt like to be a grown-up. To be a man. My father had buried his father, and soon, I would bury mine. It was a universal truth, something every man must do someday, but I would have given anything to put it off for one more day, one more hour, even one more second with my father.

When we returned to Iowa, Dad's health collapsed. It was as though he'd used everything left inside him to give us that final, wonderful week in California. As Dad got sicker, my brothers and I spent more time outside the house so that Mom wouldn't have to take care of us and Dad at the same time. Our next-door neighbors, the Abdos, were good friends of the family, and more often than not, Matt and I slept at their house. They had sons near us in age, and we would stay up late into the night talking, laughing, and beating each other at games.

It felt weird not being at home—but truthfully, it felt weirder being there. The house I knew was a place full of laughter, music, and the scent of delicious food constantly wafting out of the kitchen. Now our house was full of whispered voices and quiet tears. I could deal with my father dying—but I couldn't deal with watching him die. And he didn't want that. I knew he wanted me to remember the laughing, loving father I grew up with, the Dad who took me all around California, not the sick man who could barely walk. Mom tried to keep our spirits up, but those last few weeks were hard on all of us, but especially on her, because she took care of everyone else.

My dad died in his bed at a little before two a.m. on June 10, 2007. Matt and I were asleep at our neighbors' house. When they woke me up to say there was a phone call from my mom, I knew instantly that Dad had passed, but part of me refused to believe it. I refused to believe so hard that when I got up the next morning, I was convinced it was all just a bad dream. Even once I knew it was true, I let it touch only the outside of me. I couldn't cry. I couldn't give a speech at his funeral. Instead, I pretended I was somewhere else, at a service for a friend, or someone

I didn't even know. I understood that Dad was gone, but it was months before I really felt it.

And once I did, I could never not feel it—that dull ache of something missing, like when you lose a tooth and your tongue constantly probes the place it had once been. There is a Sam Ko–shaped hole in this world, and nothing will ever fill it. Thankfully, I know in my heart that there is another world beyond this one, and that my father is waiting for me there.

Right after Dad passed away, my mom was out on our front porch, talking on the phone with a good friend. As she stared at the moon, a star burst into glorious movement. Most shooting stars went across the sky from one end of the horizon to the other. This one went straight up, like a rocket. I think it was my father's soul, ascending to heaven.

I know that he watches over me every day. He is in front of me, clearing my path; behind me, holding me up; and at my side, whispering encouragement. He's my dad, whether here on earth or up in heaven. Nothing will ever change that. I spent all this time worrying about whether he would ever get to see me dance ballet, but now I know that he watches me every time I'm onstage.

I love you, Dad.

CHAPTER 10

Lost and Found

Have you ever arrived somewhere that you expected to be full of people and found it empty? Like if you wrote down the wrong room for a test, or showed up to a party only to realize you had the wrong date? Even before you figure out what's happened, there's that feeling of something being off—too still, too quiet. It's the feeling of something missing.

That's how the house felt in the weeks after Dad's death. I constantly expected to hear his laugh, or smell his cooking, or walk into the living room and find him tinkering with our stereo. Because everything else was so normal, it seemed like he wasn't really gone, he was just somewhere in the wings, waiting for his entrance. I constantly felt like I was walking through a maze, with my father always ahead of me, just out of sight. If I could walk fast enough, or if I opened the right door at the right time, my father would be there.

But no matter how I tried, I couldn't catch him.

I refused to cry, at least not when other people were around. I didn't want them to see me, and more than that, I just couldn't do it. When other people were in the room, that part of me shut off. I guess I've always been a pretty private person that way.

But at night, before I got into bed, I would say my prayers, and the tears would come. In my dark bedroom, listening to the quiet sounds of Matt's deep-sleep breathing, I wrapped my arms around myself and cried. Sometimes I would call my dad's cell phone, just to hear his voice on the message.

I miss you so much, Dad, I thought. *Why did you have to leave?*

One night, something stirred inside me. It was almost as though I could hear Dad's voice in my head saying "I'm right here." And it was true. I could feel him in the room with me. From then on, I knew that Dad would always be with me, no matter what. That's when I started talking to him regularly. Every night, after I said my prayers, I'd tell Dad about my day: the dance classes I'd taken, the subjects I'd studied, the funny thing that Mom, John, or Matt had done. It was a way of keeping him in my life. If I was always thinking about him, then I'd never forget his face, or the sound of his laugh, or the way his hand felt when he ruffled my hair.

One of my biggest regrets in life is that I couldn't speak at Dad's funeral. Mom asked if I wanted to, but for the same reason I couldn't cry in front of people, I couldn't imagine giving a speech. Everything was too raw and painful, and I felt like I had to hold it all in. If I let go for one second, or let one tear fall, I worried I might explode. But I wish I could have gotten up there and told everyone how wonderful Dad was, the way John did. His speech was beautiful and moving. It was like he was saying good-bye, thank you, and I love you all rolled up in one. I wish I could have been as eloquent as John, but it just wasn't my way.

But I wanted to do something to honor Dad, even if I didn't know what. I racked my brain, trying to come up with a way to say good-bye that felt right. A few days after the funeral, it came to me: I was going to choreograph a dance for Dad. But it wouldn't be just any ordinary dance. I was going to make the entire piece out of the things Dad and I did together, like riding bikes and fishing. Every step, every movement would be dedicated to Dad's memory.

I don't know how the idea came to me, or why I

thought I could pull it off. I'd sort of taken a class in choreography once before, with Michael. She called it improv, probably because no six-year-old would want to take a class in choreography, but what we learned was the basics of matching a physical movement to a piece of music. That had been years ago, though, and I didn't remember much. Also, I wanted the piece to have a lot of ballet in it, because I knew that would make Dad proud, and I didn't know anywhere near enough ballet to choreograph a number like that on my own. And the only teacher I thought I could ask—Tad—couldn't see me anymore.

Right after Dad died, my family and I went to California for over a month, this time with my auntie Kristin and uncle David and my dad's family. It felt good to be close to them. We were able to go because my mom had finished teaching summer school. When we returned to Iowa City, we found out that Tad was worried I wasn't going to continue dancing after Dad's death, because I'd been gone for so long.

"Tad won't be teaching you anymore," Mom told me after they spoke.

"What?" I asked, shocked. "Why?"

"He says he can't, and he had to take another student in your place while we were away," Mom said. I could tell she was disappointed.

I didn't know what to say. I felt lost. Tad had been the only anchor I had left in the dance world. I'd thought he was going to be my mentor in ballet, and now he wasn't even going to be my teacher. I opened my mouth to ask Mom a question, but she beat me to it.

"We'll find you a new teacher," she said. "You need a male role model. And we're going to find you one." She hugged me hard to her chest. Her strength convinced me she could make everything right.

Without Tad, it wasn't just my ballet education that ground to a halt. I was left without someone to help me craft my memorial to Dad. But I knew I couldn't do it alone. I went to my mom.

"That's beautiful, Alex," she said, after I explained the idea. "Your dad would be so proud."

I needed a choreographer who would make a piece with me, someone who would take it seriously, not just whip a premade routine out of his back pocket. On a tip from some friends, Mom called the University of Iowa Department of Dance and discovered that the Dance Forum had a new director whose husband was a professor of dance named Eloy Barragán. Mom called that very day.

When Mom explained what I wanted, Eloy asked us in for an interview. He spoke quietly and with a wonderful

Spanish accent. He peppered me with questions about dance, my dad, and my goals in life.

Though I didn't know it at the time, Eloy was a big deal. He was an amazing ballet dancer who had performed with companies all around the world, from his native Mexico to Beijing, Washington, and now Iowa City. More than that, though, he was a renowned choreographer. Just a few years before we started working together, the National Endowment for the Arts had given him a prestigious choreography fellowship.

At the end of the conversation, Eloy looked me dead in the eye. His mouth crinkled into a huge smile, his white teeth shining against his brown skin. He twitched his black, bushy eyebrows.

"I'll help you," he agreed. "And you'll perform it here, at the university, on a real stage. If we're doing this, we're going to do it right."

Like that, Eloy and I set off on the first step of what would be my new dance life.

CHAPTER 11

The Dance

"Perfect!" Eloy said, and he clapped his hands. The sound of his voice echoed loudly around the small studio, which was empty aside from us, a huge wall of mirrors, and the chair I used in the piece we were choreographing. It was September 2007, I was eleven years old, and Dad's funeral was only a few months behind us.

I'll never forget that room: Studio E103 in Halsey Hall. Halsey was where all of the dance studios at the university were located. Even though I'd been coming to campus for years—on my bike with Dad, for gymnastics with Dmitri, and eventually, to the hospital—I'd never rehearsed a solo like this before. Halsey Hall E103 was my introduction to a real ballet dance program.

From the outside, Halsey was a big brick colonial building, like the ones I imagined whenever I thought about going to Yale or Harvard or any posh institution. But inside they had carved spacious studios out of the original architecture. There were large windows to let in light, and ginormous mirrors so we could see our every movement.

E103 was a smaller studio on the first floor, and it's where Eloy and I met every other week for months as we choreographed Dad's memorial.

"I don't think this is right," I said as I thought about the movement I had just performed. "I don't think it should go there."

The step in question involved me grabbing the silver aluminum chair in the center of the room and lying on it horizontally, so that my head stretched out in one direction and my feet in the other. Once there, I paused, held myself perfectly straight, and pedaled my legs like a bicycle. Eloy and I had choreographed the movement to pay tribute to all of the cycling Dad and I had done. I loved it, but I wasn't sure it was in the right place in the piece. It didn't flow the way I wanted.

Eloy thought for a moment before responding.

"Where do you think it should go?" he asked.

"Earlier?" I hesitated. I rubbed my arms, which ached from the workout I'd gotten. "I'm not sure yet. I just know it doesn't go *here*."

"Why don't we try it at the beginning, right after the arm movements?" Eloy suggested. I thought about it, and then nodded. Biking was so much of what Dad and I did together, it made sense to put it at the beginning of the piece.

This was how our process generally went. I came in with moments that I wanted the dance to reference, or things Dad and I had done that I wanted to create movements from. Eloy and I worked together to translate the activity into a step. My movements came from everything: gymnastics, bike riding, fishing, ballet. Even things like church and dinner were part of the piece.

The best part was that Eloy treated me as an equal. Or maybe even more than an equal. He knew how much the piece mattered to me. Normally, I listen very closely to my teachers and directors and try to do exactly what they say. That's just part of being a professional. As much as art and dance are about inspiration and creativity, they're also jobs, and if you want to be successful, you've got to listen. Everyone might joke about "Broadway divas," and I'm sure they're out there, but all the actors and dancers I've ever met were complete professionals who did the work when and how their boss told them to do it.

But in this process, Eloy wasn't the boss. Neither was I, really, but Eloy let me have final say on things because this was my piece. We would try something, and if I didn't like it, we'd try something else. I'm not like this usually, but this piece had to be just right, and I was the only one who knew what *right* meant. I wanted Dad to look down and be proud. So I said no to Eloy more often than I probably did to every other teacher in my life combined, and Eloy respected me for it. If I'd known at the time what an accomplished choreographer he was, I probably would have been too embarrassed to insist. Thankfully, sometimes, ignorance really is bliss.

Even though Eloy let me say yes or no to things, he guided me through the entire process. He was the choreographer—I just had a lot of opinions. But it was amazing to work in such a collaborative process.

"Let's start from the top," he suggested, after we had a found a new place to try the biking move. "Do you think you can do the whole thing?"

I nodded. Eloy went over to restart the music. He looked back at me, raising one eyebrow to ask if I was ready. I smiled and gave him a thumbs-up as he hit play on the stereo.

Having Eloy in my life helped me regain some sense of stability now that Dad was gone. For months after his passing, everything seemed up in the air. Mom was still only working part-time, which meant that money was tight, and our whole family was still grieving. Nothing in my world seemed solid.

During this time, Eloy was like my father figure, ballet role model, and dream teacher all combined into one. No person can ever "replace" someone else, but Eloy filled some of the space that had been left by my father's passing. He even helped me feel better about not crying at his funeral.

"When my mom died, I couldn't cry either," he told me as we sat around after rehearsal one day. "Everyone grieves in their own way. This is yours. Say good-bye to your father through your dance."

As the first notes of Yo-Yo Ma's "Back to School" filled room E103, I thought of what Eloy had told me and whispered, *"Good-bye."* Then I settled onto the chair, which sat alone in the center of the room. Yo-Yo Ma had been one of my father's favorite musicians, and the title of the song made me think about Dad telling me to learn ballet. It was the perfect piece of music for the memorial. I called it "For Ko Cheuk Man, with Love, from Ko Jun Dak." It wasn't a long dance—just about two minutes—but it told the story of my dad and me. It was a very smooth piece, with each motion flowing into the next gracefully. Stylistically, it was contemporary ballet, but I incorporated lots of new moves that Eloy and I created, as well as steps I'd learned in all of my previous dance classes, and even pieces from my tumbling and gymnastics days.

Sitting quietly on the chair, I could feel Eloy's eyes on me, bright and eager. I took a deep breath and made sure I could feel the chair stable and strong beneath me. In making the piece, I knew I wanted to be able to interact with something, so I used the chair as a prop. Sometimes it was a stand-in for Dad, sometimes it was just something for me to dance around. I spun it. I leaped over it. I lifted it up and jumped with it. I even did a handstand on it.

But as the piece opened, I sat completely still on it, facing forward. Slowly, I moved my arms up to the heavens, pointing at my dad and letting him know the piece was for him. As the music grew, my arms moved faster, and I wrapped myself in a hug, as though Dad were reaching down to me. Then I began to move faster, swinging myself over and around so I could lie horizontally on the chair and pedal my feet. Next I leaped up, balanced on the back of the chair, and reached up to heaven. From that moment on, I was in constant motion, flying around the chair to Yo-Yo Ma's graceful cello. I forgot about Studio E103. I forgot about Eloy's watchful gaze. Everything became part of the dance, and the dance became everything. For a precious few moments, I even managed to forget the pain of losing Dad.

If you've never lost a parent, it's hard to explain how completely it changes your life. I needed time to discover who I was without Dad, and throwing myself into working with Eloy gave this to me. It was a way to think about Dad without feeling miserable or lost. Creating that dance was what helped me get through the long months following Dad's funeral. I don't remember much else from that time besides working with Eloy. It seemed almost as if I walked into Halsey Hall for that first meeting, began dancing, and the next thing I knew, six months had passed and I was onstage at the university, looking out at the crowd as the last notes of the music faded.

"That was amazing," Mom said as I ran offstage, suddenly shy. Tears were streaming down her cheeks.

"Alex!" Eloy clapped me on the back. "That was beautiful. Beautiful! All the other dance faculty are buzzing about my new prodigy."

"Really?" I said, shocked.

"Just you wait. I'm going to have to fight to keep you!"

I'd expected the dance to mean something to people who'd known Dad, but I had no idea strangers would be interested, let alone impressed. But I guess that shows that when you make something from pure love, and you work on it as hard as you can, it shines with a brightness that is undeniable. No matter how far I go in life, that performance will remain the most important dance I've ever done.

And while it helped me grieve for Dad and move forward, it also had another big impact on my life that was less psychological and more practical. After working together on the piece for a few weeks, Eloy and his wife, Sarah, invited me to join the Dance Forum at the University of Iowa.

"Spring semester starts in January," he told my mom. "I think Alex is ready—though it won't be easy, especially with your busy schedule. The program is very demanding."

"I want to do it," I said without hesitation. I'd been looking for a real ballet teacher so I could make Dad proud. I knew in my heart that Eloy was the one.

"You're sure about this, Alex?" Mom asked. I nodded so hard, I looked like one of those bobble-head toys.

"Then we'll do it. I'll make it happen," she said.

I knew it wouldn't be easy to get the money, but Mom made it happen, and in January of 2008, I officially became a student at the Dance Forum at the University of Iowa.

As a novice ballet dancer, I knew I'd have to prove

myself. Thankfully, I was ready for the challenge. As soon as I started, I was there nearly every day. I had a lot of ground to make up. I was blessed with a great gift, but no matter how talented you are, you can't get far without training. I was determined to show to everyone—Eloy, Sarah, Mom, Dad, myself—that I could make it as a professional ballet dancer.

I worked constantly on my turnout and my point, training my body to stretch into the difficult shapes that ballet requires. Whenever I stood around, I did so in what we called "froggie position," with my feet pointed out and my legs slightly bent. Eloy built me a wooden device to improve the arch of my foot, which was like a board that I pressed my toes against. I carried it in my bag at all times. Every spare moment was spent getting my body ready for ballet.

Once I was ready, Eloy said, the next step would be to find a professional company to take me on for the summer. Studying with a school like Pacific Northwest Ballet or the Kirov was how you got people to notice you, and began the long process of becoming a company member.

There was only one catch: it was already January. Auditions for summer programs were in just a few weeks. Aside from my short time with Tad, and my private lessons with Eloy, I'd barely had any real training in ballet. I could show all the promise and raw talent in the world, but if I didn't have the technique, no one would take me.

The clock was ticking.

CHAPTER 12

So Close

"Take this," the young woman at the desk said, handing me an index card with the number sixty-seven on it. She looked bored and tired. I couldn't blame her. It was well after seven p.m., and judging from the roomful of people around us, she'd been working nonstop.

"Put it on," she continued without looking up from the paper in front of her. I couldn't read the sheet upside down, but it was obviously a list of names. She checked off what was probably mine (there weren't a lot of two-letter entries on the list) and looked up. She seemed surprised to see I was still there.

"This is my first time," I said, looking at the index card. "What do I do with this?"

"The teachers use them to identify you for scoring purposes," she said. "Put it on like this."

She grabbed the card back from me.

"Oops," she said. "Sorry, I see the problem now. This fell off."

She held up a silver safety pin. With two quick pokes, she put the pin through the card and attached the card to my unitard.

"Good luck." She smiled at me.

It was the last smile I saw all night.

I was at the studio of the Joffrey Ballet in Chicago, auditioning for the Kirov Academy of Ballet in Washington, D.C., which is an extremely prestigious school affiliated with the Kirov Ballet in Russia. It was exciting just to be standing on the same floor that so many famous dancers had trained on, sweated on, and (if their feet were anything like mine) bled on.

Exciting, and a little intimidating. This was my first time auditioning for a big ballet school. In fact, aside from when I "auditioned" at Nolte for a part in *The Nutcracker*, it was my first real ballet audition ever.

Eloy had spent a lot of time prepping me for it.

"This is the season of ballet auditions," he told those of us in the Dance Forum. "You might go on five or ten auditions for some of the most prestigious companies in the country. They're only going to take thirty or forty or fifty dancers, total, so you've got to stand out. Be prepared, be happy, be amazing."

Because we were in Iowa, the closest place to audition was Chicago, which was a few hours' drive away. I tried to schedule my auditions so that I could do two or three in one day, because it cost money every single time we went. I desperately wanted to attend a summer program, because that's how you eventually get invited to join a company, the goal of most professional ballet dancers. But we were going to have to save a lot of money to make that happen. Tuition alone was close to two thousand dollars at most of them, and that didn't include housing, food, transportation, etc. It could end up being four, five, or six thousand dollars total for just a few weeks of training. I had as much chance of getting that much cash together as I did of growing wings.

I shook my head, trying to drive away thoughts about money. I looked around the lobby, which was full of other kids my age. There were probably fifty of us crowded into the room, and this was only one of the Kirov's many audition times. There must have been hundreds of us trying out in Chicago alone, not to mention all the other applicants in other cities. The competition was going to be tough. Not only did I need to get into a program, I needed to get a scholarship—scholarships are unicorn rare. I needed to be my best, which was a lot to ask after only a few months of training. So to have decent odds, I tried out for a dozen different schools. Surely, I figured, one of them would give me a scholarship.

"Everyone!" a man at the front of the room barked. He had a clipboard in one hand, and it was obvious he was a trained dancer. He had a rough Russian accent (which made everything he said that much more intimidating), and he wore a black unitard.

"Come with me," he said.

He ushered all of us into a beautiful studio and had us line up in rows with our numbers facing forward. For the first time in my dance career, I was in a room with a bunch of other boy ballet dancers. It was strange to see so many other guys like me, and it made me both excited and nervous. Excited, because there were never guys to talk to in any of my classes, and nervous, because each of them was my competition.

"We're going to run you through a normal class," the dance captain told us. I could feel myself starting to sweat with worry. Why did I have to pick the Kirov, one of the top companies *in the world*, for my first audition? Couldn't I have picked an easier company, or at least one that was less . . . Russian? Russian-style ballet is known for being very strict, and of all my auditions, this would probably be the toughest.

"Just do your best to follow," he continued. "If you are accepted into our summer program, this is what it will be like. Now let's begin."

Quickly, he began to lead us through our paces, showing us simple moves and combinations. We started at the barre for about forty-five minutes, where we went through pliés, *tendus*, and *fondus* (not the melty-cheese thing, but a ballet move where you lower yourself by bending one knee). Then we moved to the center of the room, where we did more adagios and *tendus*, but focused on jumping and turning. A few company members sat at a table in the front of the room holding clipboards. They took notes on our performance, and I could see them occasionally conferring or pointing out a specific dancer. They stared at us so intensely, it was hard not to be intimidated.

"Do your best," Eloy had said, over and over again. "Don't worry about the rest."

That was easy for him to say—he wasn't being stared down by a group of judges! Still, I knew he was right. I made sure that my number was pinned prominently on my chest so they wouldn't miss it. After that, I tried to forget they were there and focus on the dancing. One of my biggest worries was that the Kirov taught Vaganova, or Russian-style ballet, which focused on strength and endurance. People call it a very "masculine" style. I'd never studied Russian ballet. Tad had taught Bournonville, which was a French-Russian hybrid that was more delicate and had smaller movements than Vaganova. At the Dance Forum, we focused on Balanchine, which had a lot more drama and flair. I know a lot of teachers don't approve of a student being taught two different methods at the same time, but I liked it. I got to do things in new ways. The differences were subtle but interesting. In the long run, being trained in many styles would help me, but I worried that it might be confusing at first. There was nothing I could do about it now, so I just trusted that the teachers could see my skill, regardless of my method.

The worst part about the audition wasn't the difference in style, or the stone-faced judges, or having to spend all Saturday driving to and from Chicago. The worst part was that you didn't get the results for weeks. When my audition at the Kirov finished, they thanked us all for coming and told us they would be in touch . . . eventually. Over the next week, I repeated the audition process eleven more times with different companies. I thought it would get easier, but it was always intimidating. I wanted to get in so badly. But if auditioning was bad, waiting for the results was worse. I felt like I would never find out.

Sadly, this is normal. Whether it's for a ballet school or a Broadway show, professional-level auditions can drag on and on. The worry and the wonder are always in the back of my mind. I think it's because I know that someone somewhere is judging me. When I'm in the audition, I can do better, try harder, change my form. But once it's over, I'm powerless to change anything.

Luckily, I had a lot to distract me. I loved being in classes at the university. For the first time, I wasn't the only kid who was crazy-dedicated to ballet. Everyone at the Dance Forum was there because they wanted to make it, and were willing to put in the time. It felt nice being around a group of similar kids my age.

At home, we'd settled into a routine. I'd taken on more of the chores around the house. When I really needed a distraction, I had my dog, Ming Ming, who was always excited to play fetch or go for a walk. And yeah, sure, maybe I checked the mailbox every single time I took Ming Ming out, but often I was able to forget about my auditions for hours at a time.

Applying to a summer intensive is a lot like applying to college. If you get in, you get a thick package in the mail. If you don't, it's just a thin envelope. When I found the first heavy package waiting for me—from the Kirov, actually—I thought my heart was going to explode. The

Kirov was my first choice. They were one of the best, most competitive schools in the world, and I had promised Dad that I'd study from the best.

When I handed the envelope to Mom, I was beaming.

"Alex!" she almost yelled. "This is wonderful!"

She gave me a huge hug.

"You really deserve this," she said. "Now, the moment of truth."

Mom opened the envelope and pulled out a bunch of papers. She scanned the welcome letter.

"Congratulations . . . great skill . . . accepted . . . ," she mumbled under her breath as she speed-read. Then she paused.

"Did they give me a scholarship?"

"Yes!" She actually did yell this time. And I did too. I jumped up and down with excitement. I'd gotten into one of the best programs in the country. Eloy told me that thousands of kids probably tried out. I felt honored.

"But it's only fifty percent of the tuition," she continued. "That means we'll have to come up with the rest."

She bit her lip, a sure sign that she was nervous about something. "Alex, will you excuse me for a second? I'm going to call Grandma and Grandpa."

I knew what that meant. She was going to ask her parents for money. I felt bad having to borrow from our grandparents, but we'd already talked about it weeks before. They'd said it would be my birthday and Christmas presents all rolled up in one, and they were happy to do it. Still, I knew it was hard on my mom, and I hated making her ask them. But there didn't seem to be any other option.

Over the next few weeks, I was accepted into not one, not two, but *all* of the schools I applied to. I couldn't believe how lucky I was. I think a lot of other kids who are trained in ballet technique programs have a hard time with auditions and being judged. The fact that I'd spent so long doing competition dancing definitely helped me. But sadly, most of the programs didn't give me scholarships, which meant that even though I got into a lot of schools, I couldn't consider most of them.

"So I can go to the Kirov in Washington, the School of American Ballet in New York City, or Pacific Northwest Ballet in Seattle," I told my dad late one night after saying my prayers. Those were the three schools at which I'd gotten scholarships.

"What do you think, Dad?"

No answer came, but I didn't expect one. Praying isn't like that, not for me. It's more about finding the answer in myself. I knew my dad loved water, and PNB was right on Puget Sound in Seattle. If he'd been alive, Dad would have wanted me to go there. Also, they were the only ones who'd given me a full-tuition scholarship. The other two had offered only half scholarships, which meant my mom and grandparents would be on the hook for the other half *and* everything else, like housing and food. Also, PNB taught Balanchine, so it would be the most like what I was already learning from Eloy at the Dance Forum.

"You should visit," Eloy said. "That's the only way you'll know if it's the school for you."

"I wish," I told him. We could barely afford to send me for the summer—there was no way we could afford a visit.

Or so I thought. . . .

Even without getting to visit, I decided that PNB was the right choice. Partly, it was about the money. We just couldn't afford to have me go anywhere else. But it was also about the city, and the program. Seattle wasn't as big as Washington or New York, and for a kid from Iowa, it felt manageable. I was going to be alone there all summer, and Mom felt safer imagining me in Seattle than in Manhattan. And the more I read about the school, the more I felt it would be the best match for what Eloy was already teaching me. Still, I wished I could go visit, just to be certain.

Right after I finally decided on PNB, the strangest thing happened. Mom's job made a sudden announcement: they needed her to go to Seattle—immediately.

"Do you want to go?" she asked me. "I think we can make it work, if I trade in my ticket for two cheaper ones."

Did I want to go? She'd have had to lock me in the garage to keep me home! I think I might have screamed aloud before I got ahold of myself.

I pretty much went right up to my room and started packing. When I'm excited or nervous, I get really bad and pack my whole wardrobe. I don't know why, but I always do. Every. Single. Time. It's like a disease. Some sort of packing disorder. I packed all the journals Dad had given me, and all of the framed pictures of both of us. But Mom reminded me that we could bring only what fit in a carry-on bag because it costs money to check a suitcase, so I only took one photo: a picture of Dad out in California, near the water, which always made him happy. He was smiling at the camera, looking over his shoulder, and I always felt like he was looking back at me from some moment in the far future when we would be together again. Even at my darkest moments, the photo gave me hope and made me smile. I take it with me every time I travel.

* * *

From the moment we landed, I loved Seattle. Being near water made me feel like Dad was there with us. I could almost pretend that the last year hadn't happened, and we were on a family vacation. Then there was the school. PNB was beautiful. It had big windows that let the light stream in, and these giant cool pillars outside the building. Mom arranged for me to take a master class with them, to see how I liked it. The teacher was none other than Peter Boal. He was a dancer with the New York City Ballet and artistic director of PNB. In the ballet world, he was famous.

The woman behind the desk at PNB asked if I needed dance clothes, but I'd brought mine with me.

"Thanks!" I said, my smile beaming. I couldn't believe it: everything was working out.

That class turned out to be one of the best I'd ever taken. The studio was beautiful. The students were talented and focused. Peter was amazing. The moment that I stepped out of that classroom, I was filled with pure joy. I remember Peter telling me that he was looking forward to having me come and train at the school.

Too bad it never happened.

Mom was waiting for me in the lobby when the class let out. She looked upset but wouldn't say why. My stomach flip-flopped inside me. We left the studio and went to a mall nearby to get lunch. After futzing with her chopsticks, Mom finally looked at me.

"Alex," she said, "I have to tell you something."

She took a deep breath, and I waited.

"I don't know how else to do this, so I'm just going to say it. Grandma and Grandpa don't have the money right now. I'm afraid we can't afford to send you to PNB. I'm so, so sorry."

I felt like I was in a horror movie. How was that possible? How could I be here, in Seattle, at PNB, *taking classes*, and not be able to go? Maybe I'd misheard her somehow.

"But . . . they said they would! They promised." I could feel my face growing hot as I spoke. Not only did I feel awful, I was embarrassed too. I hate being emotional in public.

"I know, and they feel terrible. *I* feel terrible. And I can't imagine how you feel. But we don't have the money, Alex. We can't change that. If I could, I would."

She put her hand on my shoulder and squeezed it gently, but I was numb.

"Why? Mom, they promised!" I knew I was repeating myself, but it just didn't make any sense. Why was this happening, just when it seemed like things were finally working out? I could feel tears welling up, and I forced them back down.

"I don't know, honey." She sniffed. She was near crying too. "I just got off the phone with them. They can't afford it right now, and we can't either."

This isn't fair! Part of me wanted to scream. I wanted to run back to the studio and beg them to take me. I'd live in the lobby. I'd clean the bathrooms! I'd do anything if they would just let me stay.

But the bigger part of me knew that Mom was right. Even with the scholarship, we couldn't afford it, not without help. And there was no one else we could ask. My plan was falling apart. How would I live up to the promise I had given Dad? If we couldn't afford teachers, how could I become a great ballet dancer? Suddenly everything was up in the air.

Thankfully, God had plans I didn't know about.

CHAPTER 13

My First Step to Broadway

"Today is a beautiful day," I whispered, looking at the ceiling from the top of the bunk beds I shared with Matt. I hadn't looked outside, and I didn't have anything special planned, but I hoped to make it true just by saying the sentence out loud. I know it sounds cheesy, but try it sometime. It doesn't work if you don't mean it, though. You have to convince yourself: today IS a beautiful day.

And I needed it. I was still reeling from learning that I wouldn't be going to PNB—or anywhere else this summer. When I got back to Iowa, I went right to my room and locked the door behind me. I couldn't stop thinking about everything I had worked for, and how it had all come to nothing. But the real reason I was so sad was that I had let Dad down. I wanted to be great for him, and how could I without great teachers?

For about a week, I moped around feeling sorry for myself, and angry at my grandparents. Everything was so . . . unfair. *What's the point of working so hard,* I thought, *if being the best doesn't even matter?*

Strangely enough, it was talking to Dad that helped me feel better. Every time I tried to tell him that it had all gone wrong, and I had totally failed, I could hear his voice in my head saying, "God doesn't make mistakes. Don't give up." I knew what I had to do: I had to forget PNB and move on. I didn't want to look at anything PNB, or watch a PNB ballet. In my head, PNB and I had broken up.

It took one week of being back in Iowa, taking ballet, and hanging out with Matt and John to really drive PNB out of my mind.

And then Eloy stopped me after class one day.

"Sarah and I are going to New York for ten days," he said. "Do you want to come?"

Instantly, I knew two things. First, I wanted to go. What performer doesn't dream about New York City? I probably thought about New York every single day of my life. Second, Mom was going to say no. Ten days in the big city without her? No way. She liked Eloy and Sarah, but we hadn't known them that long.

"I'll have to check with my mom," I told Eloy. I didn't want to say that I wanted to go until I knew I could actually do it.

"Check with her," he agreed. "She can talk to me if she wants. I think it would be good for you to see what it's like in the city." That's how he said it, as though there was only one city in the world. The city. "Going to New York will make you more well-rounded, and anyway, you'll have to go eventually if you continue being this good!"

Making him proud felt almost as good as making Dad proud.

I called Mom immediately, even though she was already on her way to pick me up.

"I have to talk to you about something," I said.

"What is it?"

"It's nothing bad," I said quickly. "But I can't tell you until we're home."

"Aaa-lex," she said, a warning tone in her voice. She hated when I did this.

If I knew she wasn't going to respond well to something, I tried to tell her at the best time possible. If I told her while we were still at the university, she would march right back into the studio to talk to Eloy and say no, and

I'd never get to New York. I had to convince her slowly.

The whole way home I could tell she was annoyed, but I refused to spill the beans until we were in the house.

"What?" she asked as soon as the front door closed behind us.

"Eloy invited me to New York with him," I started.

"No," she said, and turned away.

"But he thinks it'll be good for me!" I protested.

"No," she repeated. "End of story. I'm sorry, Alex, it's a fantastic offer and you should thank Eloy from both of us. But I just don't think it's a good idea right now."

I'd been expecting this, so I wasn't too upset. I had a plan. I waited a few days, then started begging.

"Please?"

"Pretty please?"

"I'll do anything you want."

"Pleeeeeeeease!"

"Anything. I'll do *anything*."

"I'll do extra chores for the next two years."

"I'll mow the lawn for the next *ten* years."

"Anything!"

After a week, she agreed to talk to Eloy. I knew it was a lot to ask, to let your twelve-year-old son go to New York City with just his dance teachers, but I could handle it—if Eloy convinced her I'd be in good hands.

"Let me think about it," she said after talking to Eloy. She felt better knowing that it was going to be Eloy, Sarah, and their baby going as a family. Also, Eloy mentioned that we'd be staying at Sarah's sister's house outside the city, which was both safer and cheaper. But Mom was still worried, and money was still an issue. The trip was a week and a half, so it would be way less expensive than any of the summer programs I'd looked at, but it would still cost money, which we didn't have much of.

Finally, after weeks of saying "let me think about it," Mom sat me down.

"Here are the rules," she said.

"I agree!" I yelled, before she'd even said another word. Her serious face dissolved into a laugh, and I knew everything would work out.

"You will call home every day," she said when she caught her breath. "You and I are planning out your entire schedule in advance so I know where you are at all times. And you're taking as many ballet classes as you can, because you deserve them."

Eloy arranged for me to study at Steps on Broadway, one of the premier dance studios in New York City. I was so excited I could barely believe it. I packed my schedule with as many classes as I could fit. If I was only going to be there for ten days, I wanted to make the most of it.

Little did I know that "making the most of it" in New York City could lead to some very big things. . . .

I'll never forget the city growing bigger and brighter beneath us as our plane descended for landing. The lights seemed to go on forever. It felt like you could drop Iowa City down in the middle of Manhattan and it would be swallowed up without a burp. I was just some kid, with little money and worse luck. Would I drown in the city, or shine bright? I couldn't stop thinking about it.

My fear and excitement grew as I entered Steps on Broadway for the first time. People in dance clothes rushed in and out, talking about auditions, rehearsals, and roles. Big picture windows looked out on the busy Manhattan streets below, and as I signed in to my first class, I watched bright yellow taxis whiz by outside. Above my head, portraits of famous alumni smiled down like guardian angels. One day, I hoped, my picture would join them.

Please, I whispered to myself (and Dad), *let me stay here. Don't let this be PNB all over again*. I was terrified that as soon as I let myself relax, it would all be taken from me. I'd come so close, so many times.

I slipped into the back of the studio, feeling shy and hoping to go unnoticed. As I stretched, the teacher watched me. He had short gray hair and small, wire-framed glasses that looked very sophisticated. He wore all black and was exactly what I pictured when I thought of a dance teacher in New York City. Right before we started, he came over.

"Alex Ko?" he asked.

"Yup!" I nodded. Eloy must have told him about me.

"Wilhelm Burmann," he said. "Call me Willy."

We shook hands.

"Some of this might be a little advanced for you," he continued. "So take it easy when you need to."

What? I thought. I knew he was trying to be nice, but he actually made me nervous. Well, *nervous* is the wrong word. He made me . . . more determined. I'd show him what I was made of.

"Don't worry about me," I replied. I must have had my "tough face" on, because a tiny smile spread across his lips, which happens a lot when I try to look tough. Before I could say anything else, people swarmed into the room. Willy greeted each one as they came. Everyone stared at me as they entered. I was used to being the new guy, but it was still nerve-racking to have so many people looking at me. I could tell they were wondering what some *kid* was doing there.

At Steps, I wasn't in the youth division. Everyone

else in the class was an adult, and many of them were professionals. I barely came up to their shoulders, but I was determined to show them that I deserved to be there.

As Willy led us through positions, turns, and jumps, I worked harder than I ever had before. When I leaped into the air, I imagined I was flying. When I landed, I pretended I weighed nothing. But it wasn't the moves that made the class so difficult. It was the pace. Compared to Willy's class, everything I'd done before seemed like slow motion. And no matter what I did, Willy kept coming over to give me pointers.

"Extend more," he'd say, tapping my leg as I tried to hold it rock steady and high in the air. Or he'd look at my feet and say, "Point! Point!"

I burned with shame every time he talked to me, but I wouldn't give up. All the other dancers were full-on staring at me, and I thought I'd die of embarrassment. I know now that having the attention of your teacher is a good thing, but at the time I thought it meant I was messing up—big-time. It made me feel insecure about my technique and what I had to offer to ballet. But it made me work all the harder.

After that class ended, I went right into my next one. At the same time, Willy, Sarah, and Eloy had a private meeting in the next room. I don't know exactly what Willy said, but it must have been good, because the next time I looked up from class, Sarah and Eloy were peeking in the door, giving me two giant thumbs-ups! Only then did I relax and really feel comfortable.

I wanted to stay at Steps 24-7. I remember wishing that life were just one big long day, in which we could dance all the time without having to sleep or eat or do homework. But one particular day was better than all the rest combined. That's when I met Ray Hesselink.

I was getting a drink at the water fountain before class when I noticed this giant of a guy wearing strange tap-shoe covers. They were made from thick, black, quilted material, and looked like Snuggies that had been shrunk down to foot size. I must have been staring for a while, because when I looked up (waaaaaay up), their owner was looking down at me.

"Hi, Alex," he said. "I'm Ray. Ray Hesselink. I teach tap here."

He stuck out a big hand to shake, and I took it tentatively. I'd never taken a class with him, and right away I was weirded out that he knew my name.

"Hi," I said, hoping he'd let me get a drink and leave.

"Do you tap-dance?"

"No," I said. I'm embarrassed to admit this, but I was

kind of a ballet snob. But Ray uttered the two words that changed my life forever.

"I work on a show called *Billy Elliot.*"

He paused, obviously waiting for me to say something.

"On Broadway?" he continued, trying to prompt me.

"Cool," I responded. I'd never heard of *Billy Elliot*, I had no idea what he was talking about, and I really wanted to get to class. But I couldn't figure out a way to leave without being rude.

"I've been watching you," he said.

Aaaand that was my cue to exit! I stepped back so fast I nearly fell over. This was exactly what Mom had worried about. I opened my mouth to call for help, but he rushed to continue.

"Dance. I've been watching you dance. You're a very talented young man."

"Oh. Thanks!" I said, feeling bad that a second ago I'd been convinced he was a creeper.

Ray pulled a card out of his wallet and handed it to me.

"Look, I think you'd be perfect for the role of Billy. We're holding auditions soon. Have your parents give me a call if you want to try out."

As he walked away, it dawned on me: I'd just been

asked to audition for a Broadway show. Broadway, like in all the songs and movies. Broadway, like where Hugh Jackman and Patti LuPone sang. Broadway, like the place I'd dreamed about for as long as I could remember.

Broadway.

I was calling Mom before I even realized I had the phone in my hand.

The Audition

Sometimes I imagine life as a big set of scales. Every time something bad happens, one side goes down a little farther. But eventually, something good balances it out, if you work hard enough or get lucky enough. Suddenly, after years of the scales tipping in one direction, it was as though someone reached down and put their hand on the other side (thanks, Dad). My life started to look up. Way up.

Not only was Ray Hesselink a legit big deal, he really did want me to audition for *Billy Elliot*. When Mom called him, he explained that the show needed a ballet dancer mature enough to handle a Broadway schedule but young enough to play an eleven-year-old. I was twelve, and while I was definitely young, the last few years had helped me grow up fast. Ray had seen me in my classes, and he thought I'd be great for the role.

The show, Mom said, was about a boy in Britain in the 1980s who lived in a mining town with his father. His mother was dead, and the family had very little money. It was a tough community, full of strong, proud, harsh people living in a harsh world. The miners' strike was a real historical event, although Billy was a fictional character. No work means no money, and life becomes all the harder as the miners fight for their safety and dignity. But Billy dreams of being a great ballet dancer more than anything else in the world, and despite all the odds against him, he finds a way to learn to dance, although he has to hide it from his father. When Billy gets sent to take boxing lessons at a local community center, he stays behind and joins a ballet class. The teacher, Mrs. Wilkinson, recognizes the talent inside him, and helps Billy realize his dreams of getting into a prestigious ballet school and escaping from his poverty-stricken town. In the end, his father stands up for him and his dreams, and encourages him to go to London and become the best dancer he can be. From the moment Mom told me the plot, I knew I wanted to do the show. Billy's life was so much like mine that even hearing a summary of his story gave me chills. Maybe I wasn't a great ballet dancer yet, but like Billy, I wanted to be, and I knew I could channel that hope and fear into his character if I got the part.

One thing that really confused Mom and me was race. Was Billy Asian? Did it matter? Ray explained to us that the creative team was devoted to blind casting. That means they thought the race of the Billy character didn't matter. "Given the talents of these kids, any doubts about their right to be in the show would be swept away as soon as someone saw them on that stage," said Stephen Daldry, the director of *Billy Elliot*.

This was June, and the show was set to open in November. Because the part was for minors, they had to cast the part with three boys, who would alternate performances, to stay within child labor laws. They already had the first three Billys, but they were starting to look for more.

After Ray discovered me at Steps, the teachers there offered me a great gift: a full scholarship to their six-week summer intensive. They were impressed with my technique and positive attitude, and getting that audition was the icing on the cake. Now I could train with them in New York and get ready for my audition, which would be in July. I had a little over a month and a half to prepare. I'd been dreaming of a way to return to Steps, and now I'd found one before I'd even left.

Peter O'Brien, the teacher with whom I worked the

most at Steps, was the one who made the decision. He was in his late fifties and had a very long, very distinguished career at the Royal Ballet in London. He was such a fixture on the New York dance scene that his image was immortalized in the late sixties in a mural at O'Neals' Lincoln Center Restaurant called *Dancers at the Bar.*

"If it makes a difference," Peter said on the phone, "my girlfriend and I would be honored to have you stay with us while you're in New York. We know how intimidating—and expensive—the city can be. But you *need* to be here."

It was a sweet offer, but Mom had a better idea.

"You're not going alone," she told me. "I'm coming with you this time, and Matt too."

I was expecting that. There was no way Mom would let me spend six weeks in New York alone. Sarah and Eloy had to return to Iowa, and we didn't know anyone else in the city. It seemed impossible to imagine that we could afford it, but Mom worked her magic. Through her old PhD connections, she found a professor in Queens who was going away for the summer and needed a cat sitter to live in her apartment. John volunteered to stay in Iowa and watch the house. He was nearly in college now, and he didn't want to leave his friends. Mom agreed, and arranged to have him stay with people we knew. Just about a month after I left New York, we headed back—and I knew if I did well this time, I might never have to leave again.

At first, the city was intimidating. Our apartment in Queens (Astoria) had so many locks, it looked like the landlord was preparing for a zombie attack. The first time I got on the subway by myself, I was on the phone with Mom almost the entire time getting directions. If it hadn't been an aboveground train, I don't know what I would have done. She was more nervous than I was.

When they call it a "summer *intensive* program," they're not kidding. I trained for hours, and when I wasn't training, I was working out, or thinking about training.

Finally, the day of my audition came. Mom took me to the Sheraton Hotel on Fifty-second Street, which seemed like a strange place to hold an audition, but I figured the casting people were from Broadway and knew what they were doing. The hotel was a madhouse when we arrived. There were kids in dance clothes everywhere, because the auditions were part of a much larger dance conference.

We found the casting director holding a clipboard full of pictures and names. After I checked in, she escorted us to the ballroom, which was a giant room with dark green curtains and an elaborate blue-and-white carpet. There were a lot of kids in this place as well, but most of them were just there to watch. There were only about twenty of us actually auditioning, and mostly it was kids from New York. In my head, I dubbed us "the wanna-Billys."

There were three people leading the audition. First, the casting director, Nora Brennan. She was pretty and blond and friendly, and she gave us the information about how the audition would run. Then there was an older man who was obviously a dancer—you could tell just by looking at his muscles and the graceful way he moved. Finally, there was a really young guy with light brown hair who was about my height. From the moment I saw him, I knew he had to be one of the Billys.

As soon as I entered the ballroom, we started warming up. We did jumping jacks, ran in place, and stretched. The whole time, I could sense Nora following us with her eyes—literally. When we did jumping jacks, her head even bobbed up and down. Every few seconds she would purse her lips and make another mark on her clipboard. We were all desperate to know what she was writing.

Then the dance coach called us to a stop.

"Okay, everyone," he said, "get your tap shoes on."

I froze. Tap was not my strong suit.

"Nervous?" a guy next to me asked. At first, I thought he was trying to make me worried. But I looked over and saw that he was nervous himself. No matter how calm someone might appear, if they're at an audition, they're probably just as scared as you are.

"Yeah," I admitted. "I'm not a big tapper."

I wanted to tell someone that before we started, just in case I totally embarrassed myself. Then I realized I was psyching myself out. I shook my head to get rid of my worries.

How can I embarrass myself? I thought. *I don't even know these people.*

That was comforting. Even if the audition was a disaster, it didn't matter. No one here knew me. After this was over, I could walk out and forget about it entirely if I had to.

With that in mind, I jogged to catch the other guys and get my tap shoes on. They weren't actually *my* tap shoes. Because I didn't tap a lot, and we didn't have much money, I used my older brother John's hand-me-downs. They were a little tight in the heel, but they worked.

"We're going to teach you a few combinations," the older man said, once we were all ready.

"Don't worry if you're not the best tapper," said the younger guy. "They're really looking for great ballet technique. And I've already been through all of this, so I know what I'm talking about."

In fact, he turned out to be Corey Snide, who had played Billy in the London production, which came before the Broadway show. He'd also played Billy in Australia, and done lots of other theater. An audible gasp went through the room when Corey told us who he was. Some of the other dancers looked intimidated by him, but I tried to treat him like any other instructor.

Learn the combos, I told myself. *Forget everything else.*

They taught us some of the hardest combos I'd ever done. I was terrified. After they showed us a few times, they sent us off to separate corners of the ballroom to practice. All around me, kids were tapping to different rhythms. I found a quiet corner where the sound was muffled by heavy floor-to-ceiling drapes and started practicing.

By the time they called us back together, I had the combos down, mostly. I was definitely better than some of the other kids, but there were some real tap wizards in the audition, and they showed us all up.

It's okay, I told myself. *You did all right, and you knew tap would be the hardest part. You just have to nail the next section. Please let it be ballet.*

"Tap shoes off, ballet shoes on!" yelled the dance

coach. I said a silent thank-you to Dad. Corey said they wanted good ballet technique, and I knew I could give it to them. I wasn't going to let Eloy or Dad down.

They put us in one long line and explained that we were to go one at a time, doing turns down the length of the ballroom. I went to the back of the line so I would have time to watch and prepare. Most of the kids in front of me were decent, but none of them really stood out. I thought I'd blow them away, but when my turn came, I was shaking and nearly stumbled. Nora must have known how nervous we all were, though, because she had us each do a few more passes. By the third one, I was nailing it. I managed to do four or five turns each time, which was better than almost all the other boys. Out of the corner of my eye, I saw Nora smile and nod as I did my final pass. Then she looked down at her clipboard and made a large check mark next to something, and I knew I'd aced part of the audition.

Next they had us put on our street shoes. I knew what that meant: hip-hop. I wasn't great at tap, but at least I'd taken a class or two in it and had years of experience watching John. I'd never studied hip-hop in my life.

This'll be interesting, I thought to myself.

"I'm going to teach you a three-minute combination,"

the dance coach explained. "At the end, you'll get thirty seconds to freestyle. Don't hold back."

Instantly, I knew what I was going to do. I might not be great at hip-hop, but I could still bust out backflips, handsprings, and aerials from my days in gymnastics.

When it came my turn, I owned my freestyle. I flipped around and around, letting the beat of the music take me away. This was my moment to shine. My tap had been decent and my ballet was good, but now I showed them that I had something none of the others had. Remember, in every audition, your biggest goal is to stand out. If they don't remember you, they won't cast you.

I hit my final landing and stuck it perfectly, without even a quiver. Sweat dripped down my face, and I knew I'd given it my all. If this didn't get me the part, nothing would. I looked up at Nora, and she beamed. She whispered something to the dance coach, and he smiled as well. Just knowing they'd noticed me filled me with so much energy that I could have done the whole routine all over again!

Instead, they ushered us into a smaller room. Right in the middle was a big piano, surrounded by a bunch of chairs. I like to sing, but I'm not trained by any means, so this was outside my comfort zone. I grabbed a seat and tried to squash my nerves.

There must have been some holdup in the process, because after they got us all into the room, Nora and the dance coach both left, putting Corey in charge.

"Sing 'Electricity'!" one of the wanna-Billys called out.

"Yeah!" said another. "Sing!"

"Electricity" is the big number that Billy does near the end of the show. If I hadn't listened to the London recording to prepare, I wouldn't have had any idea what they were yelling about. Most of the kids at Broadway auditions know—or at least act like they know—all about theater, but I wasn't going to let that intimidate me. In an audition, it's not what you know, it's what you can do, that matters.

For half a second, Corey looked embarrassed by all the attention.

"Really?" he asked.

"Yeah!" everyone yelled.

That was all the encouragement he needed. Soon he was up at the piano belting out the song.

> *And then I feel a change, like a fire deep inside*
> *Something bursting me wide open, impossible to hide*
> *And suddenly I'm flying, flying like a bird*

Like electricity, electricity
Sparks inside of me, and I'm free, I'm free

If you've never heard it, "Electricity" is a beautiful song. It was written for the musical by Sir Elton John, but I felt like it was speaking directly to me. That was *exactly* how I felt when I danced.

But hearing Corey sing it made me even more nervous. He was good. I'd had a few singing lessons, and for a while in elementary school I was in choir. But I definitely wouldn't call myself a professional.

When Corey finished, all the wanna-Billys burst into applause. I think he got a standing ovation. Right as the clapping died down, Nora entered the room. Suddenly it was so quiet you could have heard crickets. For a moment we had all forgotten that we were auditioning. Nora began distributing pages of sheet music.

Just sing along quietly with everyone else, I told myself. There were so many of us in the room, I figured they wouldn't notice if I hung back. Once I felt secure, I'd sing it at full volume.

"All right, everyone," Nora said. "Each of you will take one line from the song, and we'll go down the row singing. Easy peasy."

Oh, no, I thought. I'd assumed we'd sing in a group.

Going solo was a whole other animal. Just like earlier, I hurried to the back of the line, figuring that again, it would give me a little more time to prepare.

Big mistake. Because "Electricity" is a big number near the end of the show, it gets stronger and more powerful as it goes on. It's a showstopper, really. By putting myself at the back of the line, I'd ended up with one of the hardest parts to sing, full of big, ascending notes.

When it came my turn, I pushed everything out of my mind and did my best. Overthinking kills my performance every time. Worrying and wondering are for rehearsals. When you're at an audition—or onstage—you give it your all, no matter how nervous you might be.

"It's like that there's a music, playin' in your ear, but the music is impossible, impossible to hear," I sang.

I sounded okay. If I'd been a teacher, I'd have given myself a solid B.

Luckily, after the first time through, we switched lines and did the song a couple more times, so I wasn't stuck with the hard part. I wasn't the best, but I wasn't the worst, and I'd shown them that I could handle the singing and rock the dancing. The show was about a dancer, so that had to count for more. At least, that's what I told myself.

"Pass the sheets back," Nora said after about thirty

minutes. "This was wonderful. You all did a great job. We'll call you again if we want to see more of you."

And just like that, they'd ushered us back into the lobby. I couldn't believe how quickly it went. I spotted Mom and hurried over. She wasn't a stage mom, and normally she didn't stick around for my auditions, but this time I'd asked her to stay because I was so nervous.

"How was it?" Mom asked.

"Really good!" I told her. Then I thought about it for a second. "I mean, I think I did good. I think? I don't know."

The more I thought about it, the more nervous I got. Had I done well? I knew the gymnastics had impressed them, and I was pretty sure my ballet technique was spot on. But the rest . . .

"I'm sure you did well Alex," Mom said, ruffling my hair. I wanted to believe her, but she was my mom, so she had to say that.

"Excuse me?" a voice said from behind us. I turned to see Nora standing by Mom's shoulder.

"Are you Alex's mom? I'm Nora—Nora Brennan, the casting director for *Billy*. Your son is darling."

"Thank you," Mom said as they shook hands.

"Can we use some footage of Alex from the audition for press purposes?"

"Of course!" Mom said. My head was nodding so fast,

I thought it might fall off.

"Wonderful!" Nora smiled at me. She had us sign a few forms, and then left to talk to some of the other kids. "I'm very glad we met," she said.

I was too. And I hoped I'd see more of her soon.

"That's a great sign," Mom whispered as Nora walked away. "They must want you. I bet we hear from them soon."

I felt so proud, I thought I'd explode. I wanted to race home and sit by the phone until they called.

Thankfully I didn't, because I would have been sitting there for a very long time.

Callbacks

After the *Billy* audition, my days in New York went like this:

Get up, check my messages, train at Steps, check my messages, go home, work out, check my messages, have dinner with Mom and Matt, pray, talk to Dad, check my messages. If I could have checked my messages *in* my sleep, I would have.

Even though I was going crazy. I loved my classes at Steps. Every day I felt like a better dancer: a little more flexible, a little stronger, a little steadier. No matter what happened with *Billy*, coming to New York had been good for me.

"I don't think I got the part," I said to Dad late one night. "It's August, and we head home next week. If they wanted me, I'd have heard."

I decided to let it go. It was enough, for now, to have been asked to audition. Next time, I'd be better prepared.

Still, I couldn't help but be sad. It's funny how your expectations change. When I couldn't afford PNB, all I wanted was a scholarship to a summer program somewhere. But once Broadway was on the horizon, it was hard to settle for anything else. I tried to be happy with the gifts I had been given, but it took a while to accept.

When we got back to Iowa, I avoided talking about *Billy Elliot*. Instead, I threw myself back into my regular routine with Eloy at the Dance Forum. I'd improved so much while I was gone that Eloy recommended the university accept me as a student in the dance department. In September, I became the youngest person ever admitted to the University of Iowa in any major. I have to admit, that felt pretty good. Maybe not Broadway good, but not too shabby. Plus it technically means I got into college before John did, which was a great thing to be able to rub in his face when we argued.

"You deserve this," Eloy said as he handed me my shiny new college ID. "Now put that audition aside and focus."

I took Eloy's advice and pretty much forgot about *Billy Elliot*. Then one night in October the phone rang during dinner.

"Got it!" I yelled, expecting Sasha on the line. But the caller ID listed an unknown 212 number, and 212 was the area code for Manhattan.

"Mom!" I yelled, tossing the phone to her. "It's them! I think it's them!"

"Hello?" Mom answered. "Oh, yes. Of course. Hi."

For the next ten minutes, I scrunched myself into my chair and listened as Mom said, "Uh-huh. Yes. Of course! I'll tell him," and similar things. I couldn't make out a word from the other end of the line, but it had to be the people from *Billy Elliot*, I just felt it. I was so desperate to know what was going on that I texted Mom.

What r they saying? I wrote, but when I heard her cell buzz in the other room, I knew I'd just have to wait.

When Mom finally hung up, I exploded out of my chair.

"What was it? Who was it? Was it them?!"

"You're not going to believe this," Mom said.

"I got the part!" I yelled.

"No."

I stopped jumping.

"Then . . . why'd they call?"

"They want you back for a second audition! They're still interested."

"YES!" I went back to jumping, though not quite as high this time.

"They want you to prepare a solo," Mom said, and she smiled. I knew we had the same thought: my solo for Dad. I couldn't imagine a more appropriate piece to do for this audition, and I'll never forget a single step of the choreography as long as I live. It was perfect.

After that phone call, I had so much nervous energy, I didn't sit still for more than five minutes in the next month. Which was good, because I needed to spend every moment preparing. Mom called all our relatives and friends to tell them the good news and declared an early Christmas. For my present, she gave me tap-dancing and singing lessons. I wasn't going to be caught off guard again!

Or at least, I wasn't going to be caught off guard by the audition. Getting there, however, nearly proved impossible.

Moneywise, we were at one of the lowest points we'd ever been. In fact, we had to cash in everything Dad left us just to be able to afford the lessons and the trip. The show paid for our hotel, but everything else was on us. Because my solo depended on having the chair, I had to bring it with me, which added another expense. But we didn't have the money to ship it. Instead, the morning of my return to New York found me carrying a giant cardboard box to the airport. We decided to pass it off as my luggage.

As we got to the airport, one of the porters came running over to help us.

"It's okay," Mom said. "We can manage."

But I knew the truth: we didn't have the money to tip him. Mom had budgeted this trip literally down to the last dollar, and we couldn't afford extra expenses.

"What's that?" the woman behind the United Airlines counter asked when she saw my box. Her name tag read *Gayle.*

"It's my luggage," I mumbled, embarrassed already.

"Your luggage? Oh, no." Gayle began shaking her head, her long black curls flying. "That will never fit. Sorry, can't take it."

Above her head, a giant digital clock read 8:17 a.m. Our flight was in less than an hour, and the audition was first thing tomorrow. If I couldn't get the chair on the plane, there was no point in *me* getting on the plane, because without the chair, I had no solo.

Oh, no, I thought. *It's happening again.* It was all going to fall apart. Somewhere, a giant set of scales was slipping out of balance, I could feel it. I started breathing heavily. I looked at Mom in shock. In all our planning, we hadn't prepared for this. Behind us, a long line of passengers was forming. I could hear them grumbling loudly. I looked at Gayle. In her crisp white United uniform, she looked so official. There had to be some way she could help me.

"I . . . I need it," I said. I could feel my tears welling up. "Please. Is there anything I can do?"

Gayle looked at the line behind me, then at her screen, and let out a long sigh. I was certain she'd say no. Then she looked at me—really *looked* at me—and wavered. I tried to seem as pitiable as possible.

"Oh, fine!" Gayle said, and began pulling things out of a drawer beneath her computer. "What's in the box? Do we have any room to maneuver?"

"It's a chair," I said.

Gayle gave me the side eye.

"It's a long story," I said. "It's for a competition, kind of. I'd tell you, but—"

"I know, I know," Gayle responded. "Gotta make the plane."

She pushed scissors, a roll of packing tape, and a ball of twine my way.

"See this sign?" She pointed to a large poster with suitcases drawn on it. "Your box has to be smaller than these. You got fifteen minutes. Get cutting. Next!"

I grabbed those scissors so fast, it was like I was on *Project Runway*. Mom and I wrestled the box to the ground and started slicing. Other passengers had to file by us to reach the counter, but we ignored them. The whole airport could have watched and I wouldn't have cared. The only thing that mattered was that box. Come hell, high water, or TSA regulations, I was bringing that chair to New York City.

By the time I was done, the cardboard was so cut up it looked like the box of Frankenstein. But Gayle pronounced it small enough to fit and gave us our boarding passes.

"Hey!" she yelled as we walked away. "Whatever you need that chair for—good luck!"

I smiled all the way to New York.

Pretty much every person in Manhattan stared at the box as we made our way from the airport to the hotel. At first, I was excited to be back in the city, but the more people pointed and whispered, the more embarrassed I became. How could I ever imagine being cast as the lead in a Broadway show when I so obviously didn't fit here? If my life were normal, we'd have mailed the chair to our hotel and it would have been waiting for us when the taxi dropped us off. But here I was, dragging it around through the subway for people to laugh at.

"Hey," Mom said as we exited at Times Square. "You okay?"

"Yeah," I mumbled at my shoes. I didn't want to talk about it, since it wasn't something we could change, but Mom knew I was lying.

"Stop for a second," she said. "Right here."

"But Mom, there are people everywhere! We're in the way," I protested.

We were right in the center of the most crowded part of Times Square, which was the most crowded part of the city. We couldn't stop!

"Let's take a picture," Mom said. "Come on, everyone does it. We should be proud, Alex."

She paused.

"*You* should be proud. Look how far you've made it already. You're in New York. A Broadway show invited you to come all the way from Iowa to audition! Now get your phone and let's take a picture."

She's right, I thought. *I should be proud.*

I held that box up like a trophy. I *had* made it to Broadway—technically. I was standing at the intersection of Broadway and Forty-second Street. And it was only a matter of time before I was on Broadway for real. For all I knew, tonight I could be celebrating my first part in an actual show.

This time, the audition was held at a place called Ripley-Grier Studios. I brought a thermos of herbal tea and wore a scarf to keep my vocal cords warm on the cool November morning. I'd been so worried about catching a cold that I'd actually been sleeping with my scarf on all week.

I arrived about thirty minutes early to the audition. I hate being late for things, and arriving early means I have time to prepare myself. Usually I sew my ballet shoes while I wait, because they come with "some assembly required." Since they need to fit perfectly, you buy them in your size and then sew in elastic to get the exact fit you need. At first it seemed weird to have to sew them myself—especially considering how expensive they can be—but now I find it meditative. It helps me clear my mind before I have to perform.

The studio was divided by a big white curtain, with kids on one side and parents peeking around from the other. There were nearly forty of us auditioning. The last audition had mostly been kids from the New York City area, but the callback brought in every boy they were interested in from across the country.

Mom took one look at the room and shook her head.

"Do you want me to stay?" she asked, wrinkling her nose.

"It's cool," I said. "You should go."

Honestly? I find "helicopter parents" who hang around

their kids' auditions kind of creepy. Mom hates small talk, and even the nicest show-business parents are really competitive. I can't imagine talking to them is much fun.

That's not the real reason I don't like them, though. The kids with the most overbearing parents tend to be the ones who try the least. Maybe it's because they don't really want it, or maybe they're just used to having someone else push them. I don't get that. To make it, you have to have your own drive.

Without Mom at my auditions, I knew everything was riding on me, which meant I had to be responsible. I think this attitude is a big part of what's gotten me as far as I am today.

After Mom left, I sat down against the wall and started sewing my shoes, but it wasn't long before I noticed all the whispering.

"What the heck is that for?"

"Was he worried they'd make him stand?"

"Why'd he bring a chair?"

It wasn't hard to guess who they were whispering about. Generally, theater people are pretty nosy. Because we have to play so many characters, everyone is always trying to understand the people around them. It's like constantly doing research for a role you might get someday. At auditions, it's worse because everyone is nervous and hypercompetitive, so they like to peck at each other. Mostly I try to keep my mouth shut and not get involved, but sometimes it drives me crazy and I just want everyone to be quiet.

When one of the kids finally worked up the nerve to ask me about the chair, I told him it was for my solo and left it at that. A dozen people all asked me about it over the next fifteen minutes. It was a relief when a tall, blond woman with a clipboard walked in and everyone started whispering about her instead. At first, I didn't recognize her, but as she walked by me, she squeezed my shoulder.

"Good to see you again, Alex," she said. It was Nora, the casting director.

"Good morning, everyone!" Nora said brightly. The room went silent. "Please follow me and bring your gear."

Nora led us into another studio, where eight people sat behind a long table. Each had a pile of head shots and résumés in front of them, along with a bright red pen. Suddenly I understood how the contestants on *American Idol* felt.

"This is the creative team behind *Billy Elliot*," Nora told us. "Should you be cast, these will be the people who will teach you, direct you, and train you. First, let me introduce Stephen Daldry, the director."

Everyone clapped, and Stephen gave a gentle wave

and nod of his head. He had salt-and-pepper hair and bright twinkling eyes. His voice was soft and he had a British accent, which reminded me of Dad. Eventually, he would become a close family friend and mentor, but at the time all I could think was *Oh, wow! No pressure here. . . . Yeah, right.*

I'd done some research and found out that Stephen was a big deal. On top of the *Billy Elliot* musical, he'd directed the movie of *Billy Elliot* and the critically acclaimed movie *The Hours*. Auditioning for him could make or break my career.

The rest of the panel was impressive as well: the choreographer, assistant director, dance captains, etc. These were the people who created *Billy Elliot*. I couldn't mess up in front of them!

When the intros were done, one of the dance captains stood up and walked to the center of the room. *Click, click, click* went her heels. I looked down and saw that she was already wearing tap shoes.

"Okay, everyone, watch me," she said without preamble. She broke into a quick tap routine. "Pick it up as best you can, and you'll have a few minutes to practice while we get in lines."

I tried not to get nervous that we were starting with tap again. I made my way to the back corner of the room, slipped on my tap shoes, and began practicing. Around me, I noticed a few kids who got the routine instantly, but most needed a little time, like I did, which made me feel better. The tap lessons paid off, however, and I was faster and smoother than I'd been last time. By the time we actually performed the routine, I had it down.

Somewhere in the middle of the number, however, my left foot began to ache. Maybe I'd grown a bit in the intervening months, or maybe my foot was swollen, but either way, the shoe was way too tight. I was still using John's old pair. I hadn't told Mom they hurt, because I felt bad about how much this trip cost already. I figured it was just one more audition. But I could feel blisters forming on my foot, and every time I kicked my heel against the floor, the leather scraped my skin.

After forty-five minutes, we finished the tap portion of the audition. I thought I did pretty well, overall, but there were some amazing tappers in the room. As soon as we finished the last combo, another coach stood up.

"M'name's Kate, and I'm the show's associate choreographer," she said, with a bright Australian lilt to her voice. "I'll be teaching you a ballet routine." All around me, kids started running for their shoes. There was no time wasted in this audition. Either you kept up, or you didn't. I wanted to check on my foot, but I didn't have time to leave, and I didn't want anyone to know it hurt. They might make me stop dancing, and I hadn't come this far just to get knocked out over a stupid blister. I switched shoes as fast as possible so no one would notice the red, irritated patch on my heel.

But I couldn't stop thinking about my foot, even as Kate taught us a strange ballet routine. It was very precise and rigid, and all of our movements reminded me of soldiers marching. It was only thirty seconds long, and it ended with a long series of turns.

"Got it?" she asked after she'd run the number a few times. "Practice for five, then we'll do it for real."

Everyone started practicing the routine, but my foot was throbbing so much it was hard to concentrate. When I got to the section with all the turns, I did a few, then stopped.

Maybe if I rest for a second, I thought to myself, *it'll stop hurting.*

All around me, boys were turning and turning and turning. I felt awkward standing still. I looked at the panel and noticed that Peter Darling, the show's choreographer, was staring at me. He had the weirdest expression on his face, as though he'd eaten something bad. When he caught me looking, he turned to Kate and whispered in her ear. They didn't look happy.

My blood froze. I started turning like a tornado. The worst thing you can do in an audition is freeze. Mistakes happen everywhere—even on Broadway—so if one happens in an audition, I just roll with it. Show the casting people that you can think on your feet. Never, ever give up.

The ballet routine was actually kind of easy for me, which was a nice surprise. I'd say I did as well as anyone else in the room, and better than most. But my foot was burning, and I knew I was going to have problems for the rest of the audition.

"Great," Kate said when we were done. "You guys did great."

Our solos were up next. They brought us back to the room with the curtain and told us that we'd be here for the rest of the day. They read the list of soloists, and I was toward the end. In gymnastics, being at the end of the roster was generally a good thing. That's where you put your strongest performers. I had no idea if the same was true on Broadway, but I told myself it was, because it made me feel more confident.

"You can leave that there," Nora said as she saw me carrying my chair out of the studio and into the solo room.

"It's actually for my dance," I responded, blushing.

"Oh! Of course," she said. "Bring it in."

Well, I'm definitely going to stand out, I thought. Jacob, one of the other boys, had gone back to grab his tap shoes, and I knew right away he was going to be the best tapper among us.

Watching the other kids' solos wasn't as scary as I thought it would be. They were all really good, but I felt like my solo had been special. By the end, I felt pretty confident in my skills—it was my foot that worried me. I wanted to check on it, but I also didn't want to take my ballet shoes off and risk injuring it more. I bit my lip and told myself I could check once my solo was over. But my heel had gone from feeling tight and achy to hot and liquid-y, and that couldn't be good.

Right before me, Jacob went up. His solo was amazing. He was one of the best tappers I'd ever seen in my life. If *Billy Elliot* had been about a kid who wanted to be tap dancer, I wouldn't have stood a chance.

It's a show about ballet, I whispered to myself as his feet flew across the floor. *I've just got to show them great ballet.*

"Alex Ko," Nora called out after the applause died down.

I walked to the center of the room, stepping gently on my left foot. Every eye was on me—or well, on the chair. I nodded to Nora to cue the music. The three seconds of silence before it started were the longest three seconds of my life. The room actually spun before me, and all the nerves I hadn't felt up until that moment came crashing down on me. What if my foot gave out? What if I didn't remember the dance as well as I thought?

What if they just didn't like it?

Then the music came on, and the worries were wiped from my mind. Good or bad, all I could do now was dance.

Callbacks, Part 2

In the final moments of my solo, I leave the chair behind, gesture up to Dad, and bring his spirit down into me as the lights go out onstage. It's my way of saying he'll always be with me. Never have I felt his watchful eye and protective hand more than at the callback for *Billy Elliot*.

As soon as the music stopped, the applause began—and my foot burst into terrible pain. I forced a smile. I knew I'd done well. And if the pain in my heel was anything to judge by, I hadn't held back. The panel seemed impressed. Peter, the choreographer, was nodding energetically when I finished. He whispered something in Stephen's ear, and they both smiled. All the pain was suddenly worth it.

There were a few solos after me, but to be honest, I don't remember anything about them. I was focused on how I was doing in the audition, and how my foot felt. I couldn't wait until the break, when the dancing would be over and I could check on it.

"All right, everyone," Nora said. "We're on lunch for forty-five minutes."

Finally! I thought. I probed the heel of my foot with a tentative finger. Just touching it hurt. I could tell it was swollen too. Getting the shoe off was going to be painful. But at least we were done dancing.

"After lunch, we'll be working on acting and accents. But don't put your dancing shoes away yet," she hurried to say. My stomach lurched. "There will also be some individual dancing later in the afternoon."

No! I thought. All I wanted at that moment was to get my ballet shoes off and look at my heel. But if I took the shoe off, and it was really bad, I was worried I wouldn't be able to get it back on.

I half raised my hand to get Nora's attention, but as soon as she looked over, I yanked it back down. I didn't want to be the problem kid.

It's only a couple more hours, I told myself. I thought back to my days as a gymnast. I'd hurt myself way worse back then and still performed. That awful competition had been a blessing in disguise, because knowing I'd done it once gave me the confidence to push through a second time. *Pain is temporary*, I thought.

After lunch, it was time for our individual auditions. One by one, they ushered us into a separate room. The rest of us had nothing to do but sit, wait, and worry. I spent most of the time trying to assign myself points for the various parts of the auditions. *If my ballet was a nine, and my tap was an eight, and my solo . . .* etc. This kind of thinking can drive you crazy, but it's hard not to do it when you're stuck at an all-day audition. Let me tell you, it was a long afternoon.

I was one of the last names Nora called. By that point, my foot wasn't throbbing anymore, but it hurt as soon as I stepped on it. I must have made some noise, because Nora turned to me.

"Don't worry, be confident," she said. She walked me down a long hallway toward the final audition. I was so nervous, it felt like walking to a firing squad.

The entire panel looked up as I walked in.

"Alex, this is David Chase," Nora said, and pointed to the man sitting at the piano that took up most of one wall. "He's the musical director for *Billy*. Just follow his lead."

With that, we jumped right in. *At least we'll get the singing done first*, I thought. It was the part I was least confident about.

"Take a look at this," David said as I approached the piano. He pointed to a song called "The Letter." Immediately, I started to worry. Really literal titles, like "The Letter," tend to be difficult songs, because they're often big emotional numbers referring to something specific in the show.

A quick sight read confirmed that "The Letter" was tough. But before I could get nervous, I realized that the song was a conversation between Billy and his mother, who had died. Billy talked to his mom when he prayed, just like I did with my dad.

He's just like me, I thought to myself. *All I have to do is play myself.*

Suddenly it was as though I were alone in my room, talking to my father. I shut everything else out.

Dad, I hope you can hear this, I thought.

"Sing this," David said, pointing to the first line. He played the opening notes.

"And I will have missed you growing," I sang. My voice was firm and clear and a bit sad.

"Now this," David said, pointing to another line. He had me do this a few times with different parts of the song. After the sixth or seventh, he paused and closed the sheet music.

Here it comes, I thought. They were going to make me sing it without the score. My palms started to sweat.

"Great," called out Stephen, the director. "Now come sit up here."

What? I thought.

That's when I realized we weren't warming up. That was the singing audition. The scariest part of the entire day, and I'd gone through it without noticing. I guess the lessons had paid off.

Yes! I thought. In my head, I danced with joy.

Stephen pointed to a chair directly in front of the panel. All eyes were on me, and up close, they really felt like a firing squad.

"I'm William Conacher," said the man directly across the table from me. "I'm the dialect coach for Billy. We're just going to have you say some easy words, okay?"

"Sure." I nodded.

He explained that the show was set in rural northern England, where they spoke with what he called a "Geordie" accent. Luckily, it wasn't that different from the Hong Kong accent Dad had. Until I went to kindergarten, I sounded exactly like him, so I didn't think this would be hard. All I had to do was repeat after William.

He had me say words like *window*, which he pronounced "winda," and *about*, which he pronounced "aboot."

I felt silly trading words back and forth, but everyone on the panel seemed impressed. It was like playing a vocal game of follow-the-leader. After maybe ten minutes, William nodded and gave me a thumbs-up.

Apparently, that meant we were done, because Stephen handed me a stack of papers from the script, which he called "sides."

"Find the emotion in the scene," said Julian Webber, the associate director, who was reading with me. "Imagine what Billy would be feeling."

Because I didn't think of myself as an actor at the time, I read the lines the way I would say them myself. I felt such a connection to Billy that it seemed natural and easy.

The entire time I read, Stephen stared at the ground. When I finished one run-through, he'd look up, smile, and say, "Great. Now try it happier," or, "Great. Now a little slower." I thought it was odd that he didn't really look at me, since this was the acting portion of the audition, but the whole thing was so casual. In fact, it was the exact opposite of the big-group portion of the audition, which had been so stressful. I wondered what that meant. Was I doing really well, and so it felt easy? Or was I so off the mark that they saw no point in trying to correct me? Was Stephen smiling because he was happy, or was he laughing at me? Now I know that Stephen would never laugh at someone during an audition, but at the time he was kind of the bogeyman, and I was more than a little scared of him.

After maybe fifteen minutes, Stephen finally looked up.

"You're good to go!" he said, with another thumbs-up.

What does that mean? I wondered.

I stood awkwardly in the center of the room. The entire panel was talking to one another and seemed to have forgotten I was there. I didn't know if I should stay or leave. Thankfully, Nora was by the door.

"So . . . is that it?" I asked hesitantly.

"Oh, yeah, you're done with them," she said. "Now hurry up and follow me."

I had no idea where we were going. I'd thought that was the end of the audition, but apparently there was more.

They had me do all the dance choreography over again, but this time with music. I learned a little bit of an actual number from the show, but it was mostly the same as before. At first I was alone with just the dance coaches and Nora, but then more of the creative team filed in. I saw Stephen and Julian, but they didn't say anything to me. Instead, they kept having small, private discussions, which was maddening. I *knew* they were talking about me. I wished I could hear them.

At least I had something to take my mind off what they were saying: my foot. Dancing had made it ache, and I was pretty sure I was bleeding now. When I switched from my ballet slippers to my tap shoes, there was blood on the inside of the heel and all over my sock. But what was I going to do? Stop? That wasn't an option.

Soon, every step burned. When we danced "Electricity," Billy's big number in the second act, it felt like the electricity was going right up my foot! There's nothing like physical pain to distract you from your worries. I'd almost forgotten anyone else was in the room.

After the final piece of choreography, the creative team huddled together and whispered about me for fifteen seconds. I stood there and tried to bleed as quietly as I could. Thankfully Nora came over and took me by the arm.

"You did a great job," she said as she deposited me back in the waiting room. If I hadn't heard her say the same thing to every boy before me, it would have meant more, but I actually thought I had done pretty well, so I took it as a compliment.

Once Nora left, I ran straight to the bathroom. When I peeled off my shoe, my foot was sticky with blood.

I stretched my leg up and put my foot into the sink. The cold water hurt at first, but soon it soothed my raw, cracked skin. I managed to get the cuts clean, and dried them with some paper towels. I'd avoided telling Mom about the tap shoes because I didn't want to stress her out about the money. Now I knew I had to tell her, and I felt dumb for waiting as long as I had. Trying to work through the pain got me in trouble every time, but it's a hard lesson to unlearn when you're trying to do your best.

I put on my socks to hide the blisters and walked to the front desk to get some Band-Aids. Even that little bit of padding made my feet feel better. I'd just gotten my street shoes back on when Nora grabbed me.

"Alex! Just who I was looking for," she said brightly. She always had a lot of energy, like she'd just finished chugging a Red Bull. "Julian wants to see you."

She took me to the other room, where it was just Julian and me. Julian was blond, with spiky hair and chunky black plastic glasses. He was also very, very tall. He talked and moved quickly, and I found him intimidating. As soon as Nora told me it would be just us, my nerves came flooding back.

"Alex, great job today," Julian said as Nora left. He handed me another set of sides. "I just want to do a little more with you, okay?"

"Sure!" I said, excited. Anytime they want to pay you special attention, go for it. I knew this meant they liked me, I just knew it. Even if Julian intimidated me, I wanted to impress him.

"Okay, let's do this." He clapped his hands. "You read Billy."

In the scene, Billy's father freaked out because he discovered that Billy had been taking ballet. Even though my dad was more supportive than that, it wasn't hard for me to imagine myself in that very situation. Aside from the weird Briticisms, like *bloody hell* and *lassies*, I could easily picture myself saying every word on the page.

After our third run-through, Julian plucked the script from my hand.

"You should know it by now" was all he said. "Again."

Julian was so casual, as though taking my script was no big deal. I'd never seen the lines before, and I'd had no idea I was going to have to remember them. It was legitimately terrifying, but I tried not to let that show.

"Uh—" I hesitated for a second. What was the first line? If I could just remember it, I knew I'd have no problem with the whole thing. It was something about ballet. . . .

"It's not just puffs that do ballet!" I was so excited I nearly yelled. After that, the rest came easily. I said a silent thank-you to Mom and Dad for insisting that I pay attention in school and train my mind, because this was something for which I would have otherwise been totally unprepared.

After a few more run-throughs, Julian gave me a final thumbs-up and I went out to join the other kids. All the parents were there, except for Mom. I felt self-conscious, and as Nora started telling us when we might hear from them again, I wished I had Mom with me. I didn't want to forget any of the important details, and I could tell from the way the other kids were looking at me that they'd all noticed I was alone. I've always been better friends with adults than with kids my age, and this is one of the reasons why. Especially when you're eleven or twelve, it seems like every kid is quick to notice anything weird or different about you. Even when they don't say anything, you can tell they're thinking it. I tried to shrug it off, but after all the stress of the audition and the pain in my foot, I just wanted Mom to be there so I could let go and be a kid like everyone else.

As the other dancers and their parents began to talk over the audition, I grabbed my chair and headed for the elevator.

"Alex! Wait!" a voice yelled from the studio. I turned to find Nora running after me.

"I called your mom," she said. "She'll be here in a minute. Would you mind waiting a little while so I can talk to you both?"

"Of course."

"Thanks," said Nora. "And, uh, don't mention this to any of the other kids, okay?"

I nodded. I wondered if they were about to give me the part. My heart was suddenly pounding faster than it had during the dance numbers. This could be it, my moment, my big break.

Mom, I thought, *GET HERE NOW!*

Thankfully, she was only a few minutes away.

"Alex, what's going on?" I could hear the curiosity in her voice as soon as she arrived.

"I don't know!" I whispered. "But the casting director wants to talk to us."

I pointed at Nora, who was talking to Stephen and Julian. She nodded our way and gestured to a small room off the main studio. We headed in, and a few minutes later, Nora joined us.

"The creative team is very interested in you, Alex." She smiled broadly. "You should be so proud of him," she told Mom.

"I am!" Mom replied. "But what does that mean?"

Mom's always great about asking for the practical details.

"Well, nothing is set in stone, of course," Nora started. "But they'd like you to see the show, so that Alex knows what he's getting into if he gets cast. How much longer are you here in New York?"

Mom and I looked at each other. *Please!* I pleaded silently.

"We leave in the morning," she said, and I slumped.

"That's unfortunate." Nora clicked her tongue. "They'd like to offer you tickets to tomorrow night's show. Is there any way you can stay longer?"

Yes! I thought. *We can change our tickets. I don't even need to leave. I could stay here. You could just give me the part now. Please oh please oh please please please please!*

I'd never felt so close to something I'd wanted so much. I looked at Mom. She looked at the ground.

"Well, uh—I mean, I'll have to call the airline, but—" She hesitated. I slipped my hand into hers. Didn't she know how much I wanted this?

"But we can stay," she said finally, and I breathed a giant sigh of relief.

"Wonderful," said Nora. "I'll make the arrangements."

* * *

I literally jumped for joy the moment we left the studio. I was just some kid from Iowa who couldn't afford new tap shoes, and I was being given free tickets to a Broadway show! It felt like all the hours of training and rehearsing and worrying and practicing had finally paid off.

But I could tell something was wrong with Mom. She seemed down, even though she was excited for me.

"Why didn't you say yes right away?" I asked, even though I kind of knew the answer.

"Everything costs money," she said in a sad voice. She ran her hand through her hair the way she did when she was stressed. I guess I'd known that this trip cost quite a bit, but I don't think I really knew how little we had.

"We don't have to stay, Mom," I said. "I don't need to see the show, and it's not like they want me to audition more or anything.

"No!" she said quickly. She shook her head and smiled. "Alex, they want you. This is fantastic. Of course we're seeing the show. In fact, I'm letting everyone know right now."

The entire way back to the hotel, Mom called our friends and family to tell them the fantastic news. I felt like skipping, even though I had a blistered foot. When we arrived at our room, we learned that my grandparents had ordered dinner for us. I'd never had room service before in my life, and it made me feel like a star already. I guess it was their way of apologizing for PNB, which was sweet. I knew they hadn't meant to hurt me—they didn't have the money. But I didn't care about PNB anymore. All I could think about was Broadway.

CHAPTER 17

The Biggest Surprise of My Life

After the audition, I didn't think I could want the part more than I already did. But seeing the show on Broadway was awe-inspiring. It wasn't just the dancing, or the singing, or the acting, it was everything. It all came together to tell a beautiful, powerful story. When Billy's mother came down as an angel to wish him luck as he left for a bright but uncertain future as a dance student in the big city, it was like watching my life onstage. The moment the show ended, I turned to Mom.

"I need to be in this," I said as the final curtain descended. "I could do this. I could *be* Billy."

I didn't mean I could play the part. I meant I could literally be him, like in an alternate dimension or something.

"I know," said Mom, wiping tears from her eyes. "Your father would be so proud."

"I'm going to do this," I told her. "No matter what."

"I know you will," she said. "Because you are dedicated, and talented, and you have an angel watching over you."

We both looked up. I could just imagine Dad looking down on us through the beautiful carved ceiling of the Imperial Theatre, a huge smile on his face.

I'm going to make you proud, I whispered.

After we went home, I expected to hear from Nora within a few days. But days turned to weeks, and weeks to months, and no call came. Mom started applying for full-time jobs again. She still worried about leaving Matt and me home alone too much, but we couldn't make it on her part-time salary anymore. She even applied for a few jobs in New York, just in case. Luckily, she quickly got a second part-time statistics job in addition to her teaching position at Kirkwood College and the tutoring she did with high school students. Simultaneously, I started my second semester at the University of Iowa, and our time in New York faded into the background.

But in January, we got the call we'd been waiting for. Sort of.

"Another audition?" Mom said as soon as she hung up. "They should know by now if they want you. This is getting ridiculous."

I could tell she wasn't happy, and I didn't blame her. At first, they wanted us to come back for two weeks, which meant she'd have to find a substitute teacher for her classes, and I'd miss mine. We told them we could only come for one, and even that would be difficult. Though Mom was working more than full-time, we still didn't have money to waste. I figured the trip wasn't possible. But I wanted to try.

"Please, Mom? They want to see me again. They'll make a decision this time. I know it."

Mom thought about it for a few minutes. I could see her weighing all the pros and cons.

"It's your life Alex, and you've earned this. We'll do it if you want—but I still think they should be able to make a decision about whether they want you by now."

You only live once, I thought to myself.

"I want to do it," I said quickly. "But this is the last time."

If the creative team couldn't make up their minds after this, they must not really want me. I couldn't keep wasting money on something that wasn't real. But if I didn't try, I knew I would always wonder what would have happened.

It took a while to plan our trip. Stephen had been nominated for an Oscar for his new film, *The Reader*, and we had to work around his schedule. At first it seemed like we'd never find a date that fit everyone. But then Mom pulled off another miracle. In November, when we'd thought I was certain to get the part, she'd applied for a job at the New York City College of Technology. Right as we were trying to find a date for my third audition, the school called and asked her to come in for an interview in February. We suggested the same date to Nora, she spoke to Stephen, and everything fell into place.

Returning to New York felt oddly like coming home. Maybe it was just because I was paying attention, but I saw posters for *Billy Elliot* everywhere: on the subway, on taxis, on billboards. When I saw one right outside our hotel, I figured it had to be a sign.

Everything about my third audition was weird. For the first time, we weren't scheduled to start at the crack of dawn. Mom dropped me off at Ripley-Grier Studios a little before noon.

"Text me when you're done," she said. We hugged good-bye and I headed up to the sixteenth floor. Aside from Nora and the studio's receptionist, the lobby was empty.

Where is everyone? I wondered.

"Alex!" Nora said, leaping up from her chair. "It's great to see you."

"Thanks!" I said. We hugged.

"Ready?" she asked, gesturing toward the inner studio.

"Oh, sure!" I was surprised to be jumping right in. I hadn't even had a chance to sew my shoes. "Let's do it."

I expected a roomful of other kids, but inside there were just Julian and a man I'd seen at the last audition but hadn't been introduced to. They were sitting at a big table, in the center of which sat a massive binder with the words *Billy Elliot—Script* written across the front. I was surprised Stephen wasn't there, but I guess getting ready for the Oscars was keeping him pretty busy.

"Alex, grab a seat!" said Julian as I entered. He shook my hand. "This is BT McNicholl, the show's resident director."

"Nice to meet you," BT said. He was short, with dark hair and a big smile. I liked him instantly, which was good, because if I got cast, we'd be working together closely. The resident director is at the theater every day. The director (Stephen) and the assistant director (Julian) were technically BT's bosses, but they were often working on other things. If I got the role, BT was the one I'd be dealing with the most.

"Nice to meet you too!" I said.

Now I thought I understood what was going on. They must have narrowed the pool down to two or three candidates. These strange individual auditions were for the creative team to get to know us. It was nerve-racking, but I knew it meant I was so close. This was the final hurdle. Whatever BT and Julian threw at me, I was ready.

"Let's get started, shall we?" said Julian. He pushed a pencil and notebook my way. "There's one thing I want you to keep in mind as we do these scenes. The key to being a great actor is this: don't act."

He paused, a mischievous glint in his eye. I must have looked confused, because he laughed.

"If you think you're acting when you're up there, so will the audience, and they won't believe it. You have to *be* your character. Every moment has to be genuine, because the audience can smell a fake."

I nodded. I was excited to get acting notes from a big director like Julian, especially because when it came to this role, I knew I could be real.

Julian opened the script and turned to Billy's first scene.

"Let's start reading," he said. "Now, when the action starts, you'll be in the wings, upstage left."

He looked at me and gestured at my notepad. I was

confused. I didn't know how to apply this information to the audition. There was no backstage here. There wasn't even a stage! But I picked up the pencil and started writing, because I'd learned my lesson with the turns, and I didn't want to be the kid who didn't do what he was told.

When I looked up from the pad, Julian was staring at me with a weird look on his face.

"You know you have the part, right?" he said.

My brain exploded. There had been a miscommunication. This wasn't an audition at all.

It was my first rehearsal.

I spent at least five minutes sitting there in shock with my mouth hanging open as Julian and Nora sorted things out. Nora apologized repeatedly for the mix-up. Instantly we called Mom, who came running back to the studio to congratulate me.

While we were both in the room, Nora talked us through what being on Broadway would actually mean.

"We're going to start Alex in the show in the fall," she said. "That way he'll have all summer to adjust to New York and rehearse, without worrying about tutoring. He'll be on an intense in-house schedule, as well as working with outside singing and acting coaches. In fact, we'd like him to visit the coaches before you go back to Iowa so they can prepare lessons for him to do at home."

Now I understood why they had wanted me here for a whole week.

"Do you have a tap teacher?" she asked.

"No. But my brother does, and I've worked with her before," I said, thinking of Michael. "I really like her."

Nora looked at my mom.

"Michael Kohli. She's wonderful." Mom nodded.

"Great. Then we'll get her information from you and you'll start as soon as you get back home."

Nora paused in her speech and smiled.

"That is, of course, if you accept the part."

"YES!" I yelled. "I'll start right now!"

I grabbed the script, ready to show Nora just how excited I was.

"Easy there, Alex." Nora laughed. "We'll have a lot of time to work on this. We have some details to talk over with your mom, but how does starting rehearsals in"—she paused to calculate in his head—"three months sound?"

I looked at Mom and she smiled.

"My interview went well," she said. "So fingers crossed, that works for us!"

"Woo-hooooo!" I yelled, and bolted out of my chair. "Yes, yes, yes!" I couldn't contain myself any longer. I had to let it all out. I leaped with joy, and the entire room cracked up laughing. I knew right then that not only was the show great, but the people behind it were awesome as well.

The rest of the week was a blur of meetings, paperwork, and phone calls to friends and family. Just about half of Iowa seemed to hear the news at the same time, so my phone and Facebook wall blew up with congratulations. I already felt like a star.

Perhaps the most exciting part of the week was meeting Joan Lader, my new vocal coach. She was, without a doubt, one of the nicest people I met during my time at *Billy Elliot*. She reminded me of Mom: down-to-earth, no-nonsense, and supersmart. With her pretty brown bangs and wide smile, she would have totally fit in back home in Iowa City. But considering that she mostly worked with stars like Madonna and Patti LuPone, I understood why she lived in New York.

That's right, I now had the same vocal coach as Madonna. A week ago, the closest I'd been to Madonna was buying her albums on iTunes, and now I was getting advice from the same woman who trained her for the movie *Evita*.

The first time I stepped into Joan's beautiful studio on Union Square, it was hard not to think about Madonna's voice echoing down the hallway.

"Hi, Ms. Lader," I said, nervous to be meeting her for the first time. The arrangements had been made by the show, and Mom had dropped me off outside. Now it was just the two of us, and my shy side was out in force. I was embarrassed to sing in front of a woman who'd worked with some of the greatest performers in the world. I looked at the walls, the floors, her exquisite grand piano, and everything else in the room but her.

"Joan," she said, laughing. "Call me Joan. And you must be Alex."

She shook my hand and sat at the piano. She played a twinkling of notes, and I recognized the overture of *Billy Elliot*.

"We probably won't work on any of the songs from the show today," she said, surprising me. "In fact, we'll work on the numbers occasionally, but you'll do more of that with David, the show's musical director. I'm mostly here to help you strengthen, tone, and train your voice. So we'll be doing a lot of exercises."

She pulled out a small digital recorder from a bag by the piano.

"I'm going to record this for you to take home. Our first priority is your diction. In a musical, the songs tell the story, so if people can't understand what you're saying, it's a big problem. I want you to do these exercises every day while you're in Iowa."

She looked up at me, her brown eyes serious. "You'll do that, right?"

"Of course!" I rushed to assure her. I wanted to do everything I could to prepare myself for the role. And knowing that we weren't going to be singing any actual songs took a lot of the pressure off. How badly could I embarrass myself doing a bunch of exercises?

"Fantastic. Let's start with your position. Stand up straight. Bring your head back."

I tried to do as she said.

"Not that far."

She stood up and gently adjusted my head and neck until they were in perfect alignment.

"That is how you should stand when you're singing. Of course, it'll depend on what you're doing in the scene, but that's how your head and neck are best positioned to open your throat and let you sing out."

Because I hadn't taken a lot of voice lessons, no one had trained me on the technical aspects of singing. Joan had two master's degrees in speech pathology, however, and what made her so successful was that she understood the ways in which our bodies physically create sound. The way you position your head, where you create the words in your mouth, and the way you breathe all have huge effects on your voice and singing abilities.

"Do, re, mi, fa, so, la, ti, do-o-o-o-o!"

She had me do scales so she could analyze my singing. A couple of times, she had me yell as loud as I could.

"There's a lot of shouting in the play, and if you yell onstage like you would in real life, your voice will be gone," she told me. "You can't grind it out. You've got to yell from your mouth, not your throat."

The whole time we were doing the lessons, she gave me pointers on how to hold my head and chest. It was amazing to learn how the body really is an instrument, just like a guitar, and how you get different sounds by positioning yourself differently. Already I felt like I was learning so much, and rehearsals hadn't even officially started.

I met a whole lot of other people that week—more than I could keep straight! By the time I left for Iowa, I had the script (covered in notes from BT), the tape from Joan, lessons from Ann Ratray (my new acting coach), and a video of the tap numbers to work on with Michael Kohli. It felt kind of like I was homeschooling again, only this time, the subject was Broadway, my textbook was a script, and my "final exam" would be seen by thousands of people.

I couldn't wait to start studying.

CHAPTER 18

Like Flying

"Shhh," Nora whispered as she opened the door to the theater. Inside, I could hear the music from "Dream Ballet" playing softly. During this number in the show, Billy dances with a shadowed version of his older self. It was one of my very favorite parts.

Nora and I crept down the darkened aisle and slipped into two front-row seats. Because it was a rehearsal, the house was empty aside from a few members of the crew. It was my first week back in New York, and I was about to meet the three original Billys. I sat on my hands to keep myself from fidgeting nervously.

Onstage, I watched Kiril Kulish, the Billy I was going to replace, grab the hands of his dance partner. Tendrils of fog swayed around their feet, and cool blue lights indicated the scene's dreamy unreality. The two actors began to turn faster and faster. Kiril hopped into the air and his partner spun him around in wide circles, just like Dad did to me when I was a kid.

Then his partner let go, and Kiril shot off into the sky. His body remained perfectly level as he soared up into the rafters of the theater. Soon he was whirling, dipping, and flying all over the stage. As the music grew stronger, he danced an elegant partner ballet in midair.

"Wow," I couldn't help but exclaim. It was so beautiful and surreal. That's what I love about theater. If this had been a movie, the special effects would have been CGI or green-screen, but on Broadway, you knew it was real. He might be strapped into a harness, but Kiril was actually flying.

And that's pretty much how the last few months of my life had seemed: like flying. From the moment Julian said I had the part, I'd been going nonstop. I had about a million things to do for homework: start tap and singing lessons, practice the exercises I'd been given, study the script, etc. Then there was the small matter of finding a place to live in New York, figuring out what to do with our house in Iowa, finding a new school for Matt, packing, saying good-bye. . . . Every time I thought about the list of things we had to do, it seemed impossible. So instead I focused on one chore at a time.

Dad must have been smiling down on Mom as well as me, because the New York City College of Technology offered her the job in New York the week after I got the part. Not only did that mean we could afford to live in the city, it also meant they'd hire people to move our stuff, taking one headache off our plates.

It felt sad to say good-bye to the only home I'd ever known, but in a way, I felt like I'd left that life behind when Dad died. Since then, everything had been in a constant state of flux. Transporting our entire lives across the country to one of the biggest, busiest cities in the world somehow felt more stable than my previous two years in Iowa. At least now I knew what I was doing, and I'd kept my promise to Dad.

But those last three months at home felt like a movie montage, a parade of perfect moments shooting swiftly past me. I got to take dance classes with Michael and Eloy and practice gymnastics with Dmitri, Sasha, and Matt. I rode my bike down Teg Drive, out by the university, and up around the reservoir. I put my rod and reel in storage (along with nearly everything else) and vowed that I'd be back for a fishing trip as soon as possible.

A few days before I left, Michael and Eloy reserved the university's new Athletic Hall of Fame, a giant glass-and-steel complex, to throw me an amazing good-bye party. More than 150 people showed up to give me their blessings. All around the room, videos and photos from my past were being shown. When I looked to my left, I was five years old and dancing around the living room to Dad's Chinese pop tapes. When I looked to my right, I was eleven and dancing for his memory. If I spun in a circle, I could watch myself grow up. It was just like in the "Dream Ballet," except here I was dancing with my past, which was about to let me go, upward and onward into a beautiful unknown. When the last guests left, and Michael and Eloy hugged me good-bye one final time, I felt like I was ready for the city—or at least as ready as any kid from Iowa could ever be.

"Great job guys, great job!"

BT's voice interrupted my thoughts. The lights went up onstage. Kiril stopped dancing and was slowly lowered to the ground. From the wings, two other boys in identical outfits emerged. I knew from reading online that they must be Trent Kowalik and David Alvarez, the other two original Billys.

"Boys, I have someone I'd like you to meet," Nora called out. The three Billys peered out at us, hands to their foreheads to shade their eyes from the stage lights. Nora urged me up, and I stood and waved at them tentatively. Even though I was technically a Billy now too, I felt shy meeting them for the first time.

"Hi there," I said. "I'm Alex. Alex Ko."

"He's the new Billy we've been telling you about," said BT. "Come up onstage, Alex."

"Welcome aboard," said Trent, reaching down to help me up. "Good to meet you."

David and Kiril rushed over to shake my hand. Soon, I was surrounded by Billys in triplicate.

"So you're taking my place, eh?" Kiril said, frowning at me.

I froze for a second, unsure how to respond. "Um . . . I guess so?" I said. I hoped he wasn't mad that I'd been cast.

"Kiril, be nice," said BT.

Kiril flashed me a winking smile. "I'm just teasing. Though you *are* technically taking my place. But it's cool—that's the thing about being Billy: eventually, we all age out."

"I guess that's true," I said. I'd been concentrating so much on getting the part, I hadn't thought at all about what would happen after.

"You won't have to think about that for a while," said David, playfully punching me in the arm. "Shorty."

Hanging out with the three of them felt like hanging out with my brothers. We had that same playful, teasing vibe.

"This will be one of the first numbers we have you work on," said BT, gesturing toward the flying harness that Kiril still wore.

"Don't worry," Trent said. "They hardly ever drop us."

Everyone laughed.

"So is this what rehearsal's going to be like?" I asked, curious. I still had ten days before I started.

"No," said BT. "Most of your rehearsals will be with the choreographers, dance captains, musical director, etc. You won't be onstage with the rest of the company until the last few weeks, when you have your dress rehearsals and put-in."

"You'll get an email from company management on Sunday evenings," BT continued as he helped Kiril remove the flying harness. "It'll have your schedule for the week. I'm warning you now, it's going to be intense."

"I hope so," I said. "I've only got three months, and I don't just have to learn to dance—I have to learn to fly!"

Trent tossed his arms around my shoulder.

"Stick with us, kid. We'll show you the ropes—literally," he said, laughing.

I think I'm going to like working with them, I thought.

"Want to grab lunch?" Trent asked. "I can tell you all about the show."

"That'd be awesome!"

"Is that cool, BT?" Trent said. "I'm done, right?"

BT looked down at his clipboard, then nodded. "Sure. But you'll have to stay in the theater."

I pulled a brown paper bag out of my backpack. "I brought my lunch," I told Trent. Even though Mom had a great new job, we were still trying to be frugal. Plus because we Billys were so young, the show had to have a guardian watching us anytime we left the theater. So it was less of a headache for everyone if I brought my own food.

"Great!" said Trent. "I've got leftovers in my dressing room. Why don't you come up and I'll show you backstage?"

"I'll wait here for you," Nora said. "I've got some things I need to do anyway."

That was all I was waiting to hear. With a grin, I followed Trent into the back of the theater.

"Have you been here before?" he asked as we climbed the narrow staircase up to the dressing rooms. I was amazed at how many little hallways and staging areas there were. It was like a maze, but one where every square foot had a purpose.

"Once," I said. "During previews. I saw you perform."

"I hope it was a good night!" he said, throwing his hand against his forehead in mock concern.

"It wasn't good," I said, and paused. Trent spun around so fast he nearly fell down the steps. "It was amazing."

"HA!" He laughed. "I like you."

All the Billys shared a dressing room, and it was nice but small. There was a sink, a tiny fridge, and an iPod connected to two portable speakers. Trent had decorated his side with pictures of his friends, newspaper clippings, and odds and ends that were gifts from people who'd come to see him after the show.

"It's smaller than I thought it would be," I said. My only concept of Broadway dressing rooms came from movies. In real life, even big stars had small rooms. Space is always hard to come by backstage.

"You know why it's called show business, right?" Trent replied. "Because all the show is in the front, and all the business is in the back."

There certainly were a great number of people bustling back and forth outside his dressing room: carrying laundry, talking into headsets, and moving props. It takes a lot of people to put on Broadway shows, and while they may seem lighthearted and fun from the audience, they run on incredibly tight schedules, where every second counts.

"Thanks for showing me around," I said as Trent pulled his lunch from the fridge. I picked at my peanut butter sandwich. "Everything's still a little intimidating," I confessed.

"Don't worry." Trent smiled. "I felt the same way at first. You get used to it. Besides, I should be thanking you for distracting me from the nominations."

"That's right!" I exclaimed. "I forgot—congratulations, how exciting!"

Trent, David, and Kiril were all up for the Tony for Best Actor in a Musical. If Trent won, he'd be the youngest winner ever. The show had received a total of fifteen nominations, for everything from Best Lighting Design to Best Musical. In fact, *Billy Elliot* had tied *The Producers* for most Tony Award nominations ever.

"Thanks," Trent said, dipping his head. I knew exactly what he was feeling, that same mix of shyness and pride that I get every time someone congratulates me. I suddenly knew, without a doubt, that Trent and I were going to be great friends.

"So how are you liking New York?" he asked as we ate.

"It's great!" I rushed to answer. "It's so . . . fast!"

"Big change, eh?"

"Our apartment is about the size of my bedroom in Iowa!" I let out. I didn't want to complain, but Mom and I were amazed at how small New York City rooms were. "And the kids here are so . . ."

"Spoiled?" Trent laughed again.

"Ha! I was going to say 'confident.'" I'd been amazed at the little kids—way younger than me—who took the subway all on their own.

"Give it time," Trent replied. "What kind of video games do you like?" he asked, but before I could reply, his eyes darted past me to the door. "Jess! Hey! Come here."

I turned to see a young, dark-haired woman carrying a pile of shoes.

"Alex, this is Jess. She's a dresser on the show—in fact, she'll probably be your dresser. Jess, this is the newest Billy, Alex Ko."

"Good to meet you." She smiled. "Welcome!"

"Thanks." I tried to shake her hands, but the shoes were in the way.

"How's your throat?" she asked Trent.

"It's great—thanks for the pastilles."

"It's my job!" Jess said. "See you guys around!"

With that, she popped out of the dressing room.

"Your dresser is one of the most important people on the show," Trent whispered to me.

"Why's that?"

"Dressers do everything. Someone comes to see you backstage? They run interference until you're ready. No time to grab dinner? They get it. If you're feeling sick,

Jess will know before you do—and she'll get medicine for whatever it is. Plus she's also the one who gets you ready for each scene, makes sure your costumes are laundered, and all that."

"It'd be dorky to start taking notes on this stuff, right?" I asked with a laugh.

"It's overwhelming at first." Trent nodded. "But you'll get used to it. Let's see, what else should I tell you?"

For the rest of the afternoon, Trent told me stories about working backstage: who everyone was, what they did, where was the best place to grab a nap between performances on a two-show day, etc. It was like the CliffsNotes version of life on Broadway. I just hoped I could get it all down before they started me in actual rehearsals in ten days. Luckily, between Nora, BT, Trent, Jess, and everyone else I met, I already knew I had some people I could rely on.

Now it was just a matter of proving that they could rely on me.

Falling Down and Getting Up

Two months into rehearsal, I danced on the real stage for the first time. Rehearsals don't usually make me nervous, since you have to make mistakes in order to fix them. But I had butterflies in my stomach for this one, because the show was filming a short webisode about me, part of a series called *Meet the Billys.* It would introduce me to the audience now that we were only a few weeks away from my inaugural performance. Although my name had begun to appear in publicity materials, this would be my first major "public" appearance. It was kind of like that first day in a new school, when the teacher makes you stand up and say a few things about yourself, only my school was online, and everyone in the world could watch.

"A-yup, you should be nervous," said Kate Dunn, the show's associate choreographer and, I'm certain, the world's toughest pregnant Australian ballet coach. She was a fantastic dancer. In fact, she had joined the Royal Ballet in London when she was only sixteen—during the actual miners' strike that *Billy Elliot* was based on. More than almost anyone else at the show, she had the job of getting me ready to dance the part. "Watch out for the rake on the floor," she continued. "And remember to pay close attention while spinning your chair. If it gets the tiniest bit out of orbit, it'll go all wonky."

We were in the warm-up room downstairs, below the stage, getting ready. It was a thick-carpeted, very red room that felt more like a lounge than a studio. Kate was putting me through some final stretches and exercises before we went up. She was just about the most demanding teacher I'd ever had, and she refused to sugarcoat anything. I liked her for it, because I always knew where I stood with her. You never wondered if she was faking or going easy on you. But she intimidated a lot of people.

"Watch your turnout," she said as I went from first to second position. "Don't get sloppy. I'll be right there with you."

I couldn't believe how completely and totally *Billy Elliot* had taken over my life. Just today, I'd already had a separate rehearsal with Kate in the morning, then gone to sec Joan for vocal practice. And I wasn't done yet. After they filmed me, I would head uptown to visit Ann Ratray, the acting coach Stephen had arranged for me to work with.

While my lessons were similar to what I'd done back in Iowa, they felt different. Kate didn't seem like a teacher, and time with her wasn't like a class. This was my job. I was Kate's coworker, not her student. Messing up wasn't an option, because people depended on me. When it came to performing, there were no exceptions for me because I was new or young. As someone said backstage, "There are no child stars on Broadway, just professional actors who happen to be children."

Children *and* athletes. That was the other big difference in rehearsing with Kate. My classes had always included some conditioning, but to do the scheduled performances each week for *Billy Elliot*, I would have to be in the best shape of my life. A typical dance rehearsal lasted three or four hours, and included more than an hour of sprinting, sit-ups, push-ups, and other strengthening exercises. When the house was empty, Kate had us do laps in the mezzanine.

"Doing a Broadway musical is like running a marathon," Stephen told me early on. "Running a marathon *while* singing and dancing. Do you know why all the Billys come from a dance background?" he asked.

I'd never really thought about it.

"Because it takes years to get into the physical condition necessary to do this part. We can work on your voice and acting, but we can't start with someone who isn't already dance trained."

As Kate escorted me up to the stage, she peppered me with last-minute advice. "Don't think about the cameras. Make your movements big. And don't forget the rake."

For weeks, everyone had been warning me about the rake. It had nothing to do with gardening. Rather, the "rake" is the amount the stage is inclined. If the back of the stage is higher than the front, it's easier for people in the audience to clearly see the action. But it's harder to perform on, especially if you've grown used to level studio floors. Like, say, if that's what you have rehearsed on for the last two months . . .

Raked stages are more common in England, and because *Billy Elliot* started in London, the stage was as raked as it could legally be. It sloped about half an inch in height for every foot in width. Any more and it would have been too dangerous to dance on.

It was dangerous enough as it was. After they introduced me to the cameraman, Kate led me through a few numbers from the show—"Dream Ballet," "Electricity," "Angry Dance." The ballet numbers were hard, but not impossible. But tapping on the raked stage felt like trying to dance on a slippery hillside. And I wasn't even in costume, and we didn't have scenery or props yet. It was only going to get more difficult from here.

"And front, two, three, four." Kate stood over me, clapping the rhythm, helping me find my way through familiar combinations on unfamiliar ground.

I tried to push other thoughts out of my mind, but I couldn't find the peace that I needed in order to let go. Worries about the show kept intruding. What if it never got any easier? What if I was just no good at dancing on a raked stage? What if I could never forget about the audience and the cameras? I had only another month—*one month*—to get ready. Sometimes, when I wasn't doing anything, I felt a tickle of panic in my stomach when I thought about how soon it was.

"Ouch!" I exclaimed as I fell on my butt again. "Sorry."

"Yaaaah, that was awful," Kate said, but with a smile that softened the blow. "Let's try one more."

But no matter how many times we tried it, I couldn't get the tap numbers down. It was like my tap shoes had been dipped in oil.

"I think we have what we need," said the cameraman

after my four-thousandth fall. It was a nice way of saying there was no point in trying anymore. I just couldn't get it, which is why the *Meet the Billys* video about me on YouTube doesn't have a single tap step in it.

"Tomorrow, you're going to pretend this never happened, right?" Kate said as the cameraman packed up.

"Yeah," I said glumly. Everyone I knew was coming to the opening in a few weeks . . . *what if I wasn't good?* What if I embarrassed myself, or worse, Mom and Dad?

Kate must have read my thoughts.

"Come on now," she said. "You had a bad rehearsal. It happens. It doesn't mean you're bad—it just shows what you've got to work on. Think on it this way: would you rather this happen now or on opening night?"

"Now, I guess." Frankly, I'd have preferred it never happen.

"See, it's a blessing in disguise." Kate clapped me on the back. "Now come on, no time for moping. You've got an acting session to get to."

"Anybody seen a Broadway star up in here?" John called from the audience with perfect timing.

"Hey, John!" Half a dozen voices echoed back the words. I didn't even think to look up, because I didn't see myself as a star—especially not today.

Everyone at the show loved John. He was preparing

to go to college at the University of Iowa in the fall, but he was here for the summer. While Mom started her new job, he volunteered to watch out for me. I was running all over the city multiple times a day, and someone needed to make sure I didn't get lost.

Yesterday, *Meet the Billys* had filmed us dancing on Chelsea Pier, which is an old shipping dock along the Hudson River that had been converted into a beautiful park. Being near the water reminded me of Dad, and it felt less crowded and noisy than the rest of Manhattan. The city had all kinds of interesting parts. We'd discovered that we could even take the subway to the beach. Nearly every weekend, we headed to Coney Island, a beachfront amusement park complete with roller coasters, a boardwalk, and Friday-night fireworks. It was my favorite part of the city so far.

"How was rehearsal?" John asked as we headed on the C train to upper Manhattan to see Ann Ratray.

"Terrible," I grumbled.

"How bad could it have been?"

"You remember that scene in *Bambi*, on the ice?" I asked.

"The one where he keeps falling?"

"Yup." I nodded. "I must have eaten stage at least ten times today." I stared down at my shoes, wishing I could ride the subway all the way back to Iowa.

"Ouch," John replied. "Well, at least it wasn't the part with the hunters." He cocked his finger at me. "Pow! Pow!"

"Ya got me!" I moaned. I grabbed my chest and laughed out loud. John always knew how to cheer me up.

"How's the acting?"

"Good!" I perked up. I'd never really had acting lessons before, and I enjoyed working with Ann. Her class was very informal. A small group of us met in her living room, which was huge. It was seriously the biggest apartment I ever saw in Manhattan. Every week we each practiced a monologue, or part of a scene. We all watched and critiqued one another, and Ann gave us specific notes to work on for the next session.

Even though Julian had said the key to being a great actor was not to act, I still needed to be comfortable onstage. Every week, Ann helped me become a more forceful, honest presence, while Julian and BT helped me be more relaxed and natural.

"Today I'm supposed to get angry," I told John.

"Angry?"

"Ann's helping me work on being bigger onstage. I need to get over being shy."

"How?" John asked.

"Well . . ." I blushed.

"Tell me!" John blurted out as soon as he realized I was embarrassed.

"Last week she made me stand on a chair in the center of the room and swear as loudly as I could!" I felt my cheeks go red. "She made me say every curse word in the show, and more."

Although some of it has been rewritten, when I first started the show, Billy had to say a bunch of curses. Some were just British slang, which sounded worse than they were. But there were some words in the show that I never would have said in real life.

"It's not you, Alex," Ann told me when I confessed that I was having a hard time. "It's a character. You're not saying these things. *Billy* is. Don't forget that."

I guess that's the heart of acting: learning to be natural while being someone else. It's a strange road to walk. Too far to one side, and you seem fake. Too far to the other, and you're not acting.

"Here we are," John said as we got off the subway by Ann's building. "Mom'll be waiting when you're done. Good luck!"

The other actors were sitting on the couches in Ann's bright yellow living room when I entered.

"Let's get started," Ann said, pushing a stray strand of red hair behind her ear. "Alex, you're working with

Mike today. I want you to get in a fight."

Class always started with improv, to get us warmed up. After that, we worked on our scenes. I liked improv a lot. In fact, it was probably my favorite part of the class, because we did something new every week.

Mike was a big guy, like six feet, and he was probably around my dad's age. I eyed him as we walked to the center of the room. Without a word, he jumped into the scene.

"What're you doing here, huh, kid?" he said. Mike was usually a nice guy, but tonight his voice had a mean, ugly edge to it.

"None of your business! I'm—uh—you got a problem with me?"

"Yeah, I got a problem with you!" Mike stepped closer. He towered over me, much like my dad in the show did. I forced myself not to step back. "You need to get the hell out of here."

"Why should I listen to you?" I said. To my left, I could see Ann waving her hands. *More energy*, her gesture said. *Bigger!* "*You* get out of here!"

"Oh, so you want to take this outside, huh?" Mike roared.

"Stop it!" I yelled back. "You don't scare me you—you—you *butthead*!"

It was the only bad word I felt comfortable saying in

public, but I yelled it as loudly as I could. Mike actually stepped back.

"Well done, guys!" Ann interrupted us, putting a hand on each of our shoulders. "Good job, Mike. Alex, you really pushed through tonight."

"Thanks, Ann," said Mike, turning back into the nice, quiet guy I knew from class. "That was great, Alex."

"You too," I told him. "You really committed to it."

Commitment was one of the things we talked about a lot in acting class. If you're going to do something, don't go halfway. In live theater, the audience could be all the way up in the balcony, so you have to be big.

For the rest of class, I practiced a few of the angriest scenes from *Billy*. At the end, Ann pulled me aside.

"You open in a month, right?"

I nodded.

"Scared?"

"A little," I admitted.

"Don't be." Ann smiled. "You're doing great. Tell BT I think you only need to come once a week from now on."

"Really?" I said. I'd been seeing her three or four times a week since I got back to New York. If she thought I just needed one session a week, maybe I was more prepared than I thought. Maybe this day wasn't a total failure after all.

"But I want you to continue working on your cursing." She smiled. "Now go on—your mom got here early and she's waiting."

Ann had a sitting room that doubled as a waiting area. When I ran out, Mom was there, tapping away on her phone—she rarely wasted a free minute, and with her new job, she was constantly busy. We had that in common.

"Hey, Alex!" Mom looked up from the screen as I ran in.

"How was your day?" I asked.

"Long," she replied. "But good." Her new job was tough, but she loved a challenge. "How about you?"

I sped through everything that had happened, eager to tell her what Ann had said.

"And I only have to come once a week!" I said with a smile. "I think I'm getting it." After the disastrous dance rehearsal, this was exactly what I needed.

"That's great . . ." Mom paused, a mischievous smile on her face. ". . . *Butthead!*"

I blushed. "You got here really early, huh?"

"Yup," said Mom. "Early enough to hear you be excellent. I'm so proud of you Alex, and I know your dad would be too."

I smiled the whole way home. Bring on Broadway. I was ready.

Well, almost.

CHAPTER 20

In and Out

Little by little, opening night crept closer. I was fitted for costumes and had publicity photos taken. The summer ended. John went off to college, and I entered tutoring again. For the first time in a while, I was in "school" with other people—the other Billys in the show. To meet our educational requirements, we had to do a certain amount of tutoring per month, so company management provided us with teachers and space at Ripley-Grier Studios. Given our packed schedules, it made sense to do as much as we could in the same place where we rehearsed.

At one of the first sessions in September, I arrived at Ripley-Grier to find the room empty except for a guy about my age who had dusky skin and thick, curly black hair. He slouched comfortably in one of the chairs, tapping a pen on the arm.

"Hi," he said, leaping up to shake my hand as I entered. "I'm Liam Redhead."

He said it as though he expected me to know who he was, but I had no clue. My eyes drifted up to his hair, which was anything but red.

"You're—"

"Not a redhead." He smiled. "I know."

"I was going to say, you're in the show?"

"I'm playing Billy!" he responded proudly.

"Me too." I smiled. I'd heard there were new Billys coming, but I didn't know they'd already been cast. It would be nice not to be the new kid anymore. "I'm—"

"I know you!" Liam interrupted. That's how he was, always full of energy and bursting in a million directions. "You're Alex Ko! I watched the *Meet the Billys* video on you."

I blushed. "Ugh," I said. "I was a mess that day!"

"What *what*?" Liam laughed. "You were awesome! So what do I have to look forward to?"

For a second, I had a weird feeling of déjà vu. This was just like me with Trent two months ago, except now I was the one answering the questions. *How quickly things change around here!* I thought. One minute I was the new kid, and the next I was the old hand.

"It's intense," I started. "*Really* intense."

I told Liam all about the rehearsal process, or what I knew of it so far. In return, he told me that he was from Canada, had never been on Broadway before, and was mostly a dancer, not an actor. I was excited we had that in common. At first, I found Liam kind of pretentious, but within minutes I realized he was just excited and nervous. By the time our tutor showed up, he and I were fast friends. Of all the Billys on the show, he was the one I was closest to.

I never knew who I would run into while doing things for the show. Once, in between rehearsals, I heard some of the ballet girls whispering backstage.

"She was the voice of Princess Jasmine!" said one of the younger girls, giggling.

I looked where she pointed. A tiny, beautiful Filipino woman stood serenely talking to one of the male dancers. If she really was Princess Jasmine, I *had* to go introduce myself. I'd grown up watching *Aladdin*!

"Hi," I said to the woman's back, "Excuse me, but—is it true? Were you Princess Jasmine?"

The woman turned and laughed. "Yes," she said. She stared at me for a long moment, then broke out a dazzling smile. "I'm Lea. Lea Salonga."

"Alex Ko," I said, and shook her hand. "I play Billy."

I didn't know it at the time, but Lea Salonga was a huge deal. She'd been in everything—*Miss Saigon*, *Les Mis*, you name it. She hadn't just voiced one Disney princess, she'd done two, Jasmine and the title role in *Mulan*. Meeting her was an honor.

"That's a tough role for someone as young as you," she said, giving me an appraising stare.

I nodded, suddenly bashful.

"Something tells me you're up for it, though," Lea continued. She reached out to stroke my hair. "Here," she said suddenly. "Let me give you my number. I have a good feeling about you."

From that moment on, Lea became a huge supporter of mine. Though she was incredibly busy and frequently traveling, she made a point to see me every time she was in New York, and she made sure to come to my opening night.

Not long after meeting Liam and Lea, I had my first dress rehearsal and started getting ready for my put-in. A put-in is the first time you do the full show, with all the real actors, musicians, and lights—everything but the audience. That's why they call it a put-in, because they literally put you into the existing show. Mine was scheduled for the last day in September, exactly one week before I opened.

The night before the put-in, Kate called me at home.

"How'd you feel about dancing at Lincoln Center?" she asked without preamble. My heart skipped a beat.

"Great!" She didn't have to ask me twice. "Why? What's up?"

"You and the other Billys are getting the Arts and Letters award from the YMCA on behalf of *Billy Elliot*. We want you to dance 'Electricity' at the reception. It's two weeks after you open."

That meant it was in . . . three weeks! I couldn't believe it. In the space of a month, I'd be dancing on Broadway *and* at Lincoln Center. Now all I needed was Carnegie Hall!

When I told Mom, she called everyone we knew in Iowa. Most of our friends and family had arranged to see my opening night, but this was a great alternative for those who couldn't make it.

"It's like I get two opening nights," I told Dad in my prayers. "And you get to see both of them."

Buoyed up by Kate's call, I sailed through my put-in. By the time my first performance rolled around, I was nervous but confident. Kate, Stephen, Julian, BT, Joan, Ann—everyone did an amazing job of preparing me.

Opening night was fantastic. Absolutely, positively one of the best nights of my life. Not just because I was dancing on Broadway, or because all of my family and friends were there, or because I'd mastered tapping on a raked stage, but because I'd made good on my promise to Dad. I had found the best teachers, studied as hard as I could, and finally, I had made it.

But that's not to say it was all fun and games. Immediately after opening night—while I was on my way to meet my great-grandmother and the rest of my family and friends at a nearby restaurant to celebrate—Stephen grabbed me.

"I hate to do this to you," he said, "but Trent is sick. He was supposed to go on in tomorrow's matinee, and we need you to replace him."

Of course, I said yes, which meant I had to go to bed immediately. I was at my own party just long enough to drink a cranberry juice, order a Caesar salad to go, and thank everyone for coming. They were disappointed, but they understood. The show, as they say, must go on.

So I danced in the matinee the next afternoon, and in the Friday-night show after that. Mom came to every one of my performances, and each felt easier and more natural than the one before. I spent the weekend rehearsing, training, and trying to beat Matt at Wii Sports. On Sundays, Mom, Matt, and I always got bagels from our favorite bakery. As I sat at our small dining table smearing cream cheese on a toasted cinnamon-raisin bagel, Mom looked at me.

"You're scheduled for the Wednesday matinee this week," she said. "How do you feel about it?"

"Great! They've been giving me notes, but so far everyone says I'm doing really well."

"That's awesome!" said Matt. "*I* liked it."

"If you're feeling comfortable, I might not come to this performance," Mom said. "But only if you feel okay with that."

"That's cool," I told her. I'd known it would happen sooner or later, and I felt ready.

Mom looked at me with a doubtful eye.

"No, really, Mom. It's fine."

"If you say so," she replied. "But call me as soon as you get out. I want to hear all about it."

"Break a leg." Matt laughed. "Or, well, don't."

Mom rubbed Matt's head as I devoured my warm, freshly baked bagel.

It was the little moments like this that made me miss Dad the most. Sometimes I dreamed he was just in the kitchen pouring himself some coffee. I'd catch myself listening for his footsteps, or wondering why he was taking so long, and then I'd remember. If someone had told me two years ago that one day I'd forget that he was gone,

I'd have thought they were crazy. But you can't stay sad forever. At some point, the huge ball of hurt and loss that I carried inside me had dissolved. It was only after those moments when I entirely forgot Dad had passed that it all came rushing back.

"You miss him, don't you?" Mom said quietly, her bagel forgotten on her plate. She put her hand on top of mine. "Remember, he's always with you. Whether things are at their best or at their worst. He's here." She tapped my chest, right above my heart.

"I know," I said. "I just . . . wish he were here the way he used to be."

"Me too." Mom sighed. "But at least we have each other."

"Yeah," said Matt, putting his little hand on top of ours. "And a Wii."

We all laughed and my sadness passed. But Mom's words would soon be tested in a way none of us could foresee.

On Wednesday, I arrived at the theater a little before twelve thirty, or, as they say on Broadway, "an hour before half." *Half* means the thirty minutes right before the show starts. If you're called, you have to be at the theater an hour before that. So for a two-p.m. matinee, I had to get there at twelve thirty.

"Hey, Alex." Robbie, from the ensemble, greeted me backstage. He was one of Kate's dance captains, so he frequently led my warm-ups when she wasn't around. He was short, but really buff, like a gymnast. "Ready to get started?"

"Yup!" I slapped him five. "Kate didn't give me any specific notes last week, but I thought maybe we could work on some of the hard stuff in Act Two, like 'Electricity.'"

"Good by me. Let's start with the acrobatics back here, and when we get onstage we can work on your turns."

We always did the first thirty minutes of warm-up at the back of the house, so the stage was free to be set up. But they made sure I had at least fifteen minutes onstage before every show.

"Electricity" was my favorite dance, because it had been choreographed especially for me. During this scene, Billy is being asked by a bunch of judges (who already don't like him) what it feels like when he dances. It's Billy's moment to shine, so Kate made a different version for each actor, to show off our unique strengths. Mine centered on the flips, cartwheels, and aerials that I'd learned in gymnastics.

But I had to go right from tumbling into a series of difficult turns one after another. Now I knew why they'd drilled us on our turns in the audition.

"Remember," Robbie said encouragingly, "spot before you turn."

I did three, four, five turns in a row before *something* happened. I heard a loud *pop!* and suddenly I wasn't moving. In fact, I couldn't move. My left knee felt like it was made of stone. It wouldn't bend it at all. Carefully I slipped to the ground.

"Alex!" Robbie yelled, frantic.

"I'm fine!" I said. "I'm fine!

"What was that?" Bonnie, the stage manager, came running from the wings and nearly tripped over me. "Oh my God, Alex, was that you?"

"I'm fine, really," I said anxiously. I didn't feel anything. I couldn't move my knee, but it didn't hurt. "It's nothing. I just need a minute."

"I heard that backstage," she said. "You are *not* okay."

"We need a sub for Alex," I heard Robbie say. "Call BT and let him know. You okay, buddy?" He crouched down next to me.

I opened my mouth to tell him I was fine and could do the show.

That's when the pain started.

Broken Dream

Just eight blocks from the Imperial Theatre is PhysioArts, where everyone from *Billy Elliot* went for physical therapy when they were hurt. Broadway is its own little village inside New York City, containing everything a show might need all within a few short blocks.

Or at least, they seem short when you're not injured. But when your left knee won't bend and there's a searing pain running up your leg, they take forever.

Come on, Alex, you can do this, I told myself. I gritted my teeth and forced my way along the crowded sidewalk. Six blocks to go.

I'd told Robbie I could walk to Physio on my own since there wasn't a guardian available to go with me. In gymnastics, I'd learned to push through the pain, and I didn't want to disrupt the show more than I already had.

"I'm fine, really. It's bad enough you have to replace me—I don't want to cause any more headaches."

I was embarrassed by my injury. It was only my fourth show and I'd already let the team down. All I wanted was to walk to Physio, get a brace, and go home to ice my knee. But every step of the walk burned, and by the time I arrived, I was worried. I tried to play it down, but the physical therapist took one look at my knee and declared that I needed to see a surgeon.

She called the show to send a guardian, told me not to put *any* weight on my leg, and gave me a pair of crutches. As soon as I saw the crutches, I knew I was in trouble.

"How serious is it? Do you know when I'll be able to perform?" I asked everyone. They all shook their heads and said it was too soon to tell. But I could see the worry in their eyes.

Todd, my appointed guardian from the show, arrived, took me to the doctor's office, and contacted Mom. She was furious they hadn't called her immediately. At first, they'd hoped the injury wasn't serious, and by the time they realized it might be major, they were focused on getting me to a doctor. But still, it took hours before Mom was notified, and everyone at the show felt horrible about it.

Mom arrived at the doctor's office right before they showed me my X-rays.

"Alex!" She ran into the lobby. "Are you okay?"

"I don't know," I told her truthfully. "It hurts. A lot." But having her there made everything less scary.

We both looked down at my knee. Underneath my gym clothes, it was swollen and puffy. I'd been injured before, but it had never looked as bad as this.

"Alex Ko?" an older man in a doctor's outfit approached us. "I'm Dr. Hamilton. If you come with me, we can look at your X-rays."

I hobbled down the hallway, trying not to wince every time my knee brushed against something. Mom walked with those hard, precise steps that meant she was angry and scared. Like she was going into a fight.

Dr. Hamilton's office was decorated with posters of famous athletes. His practice specialized in sports medicine, which is the reason Broadway shows used him. My X-rays were clipped to a light box on the wall.

"This here is your knee," Dr. Hamilton said, pointing at a spot on the X-ray. "There's a definite tear in the tendon."

He paused.

"I've scheduled an MRI at the hospital tomorrow so we can find out exactly what we're dealing with."

"So you don't know what's wrong?" Mom said.

"His tendon may be torn or it could be Osgood-Schlatters, or choirboy knee," said Dr. Hamilton. "It happens to very active children when they have repeated small knee injuries in the same place." His voice softened. "I know you're both scared, but I'm going to see you through this. Alex, you'll be out of the show for at least a week. But I can't be certain how severe it is until the MRI."

"A week?" I said. I smiled, even though my leg was killing me. I could handle being out for a week. "So it's not too bad?"

"Don't get ahead of things," Dr. Hamilton cautioned. "It could be worse than it looks. But right now I don't think it's terrible. We'll know for sure tomorrow. Until then, I want you to rest, ice it, and fill this prescription. It'll help with the pain."

Just his words were help enough. Knowing I might only miss a week of the show improved my spirits. I still couldn't bend my knee, but maybe it wasn't as bad as it seemed.

Kate called almost immediately after I got home. She'd become the person who contacted me for all show-related business.

"Well, this will all be okay," she said as I picked up the phone. "What'd they say?"

"I have to get an MRI tomorrow," I told her. "But Dr. Hamilton thinks I could be back in a week."

That wasn't exactly what he'd said, but it was what I wanted to believe.

"Good," Kate said. "We've taken you off the schedule for now, though. Let me know what he says after the MRI."

"Sure thing."

There was a long pause on the other end of the phone. Finally, Kate cleared her throat.

"If you're not better next week, Trent's going to replace you at Lincoln Center."

My stomach dropped as though I'd been punched. Amid everything else, I'd forgotten I was supposed to perform "Electricity" at Lincoln Center in a week. I felt like the world was falling in on me. I put my hand over the phone and tried to breathe.

"Alex? You there?"

"My family's coming," I whispered.

"What?"

"My family. From California. My cousin Emily was going to come, so . . . She already has her plane ticket."

"Oh, damn!" Kate huffed. "Sorry. That's awful. But maybe Dr. Hamilton's right and you'll be fine by then."

"Yeah, maybe."

There didn't seem to be anything else to say.

"We're pulling for you," Kate said. "Call me as soon as you know anything. Or . . . even if you just want to talk. Anytime."

"Thanks," I said. "I will."

I spent the rest of the evening on the couch with my leg propped up, holding an ice pack to my knee, but if anything, it looked more swollen than before.

"I guess you know all this already," I whispered to Dad that night. "But I hurt myself today. My leg. I think it's bad, but I don't know. I'd get on my knees and pray for help, but I can't even do that. So I guess I'll just wait."

We were at the hospital first thing next morning. The MRI was a giant tube that used magnetic imaging to get a picture of my muscles and skeleton. I had to lie perfectly still. With nothing to distract me, I could feel the throbbing in my knee like a second heartbeat.

Ba-boom, ba-boom, ba-boom.

When I finally got the results from Dr. Hamilton, the expression on his face told me everything I needed to know.

"I'm not going to lie," he said, frowning at the images. "This is bad."

I broke out in a cold sweat. I felt like the room was zooming in and out of focus around me. Dr. Hamilton's voice seemed to come from far away. I grabbed Mom's hand to keep myself from fainting.

"You've torn about fifty percent of the tendon in the knee," he said. "Healing could take a while."

"How long?" I asked, my voice tight.

"I can't say. A month? A year?"

A year? My heart dropped to the floor. I felt like crying.

"What about the show?" Mom asked. "What will happen to him?"

"You'll have to ask them," Dr. Hamilton said. "But he's going to be out for a while. And he won't be able to rehearse either. Nothing that might stress his knee."

Kiril's words from when we first met came floating back to me: *"Eventually, we all age out."* I was thirteen, going on fourteen. Billy was supposed to be eleven. In a year, would I still be able to play the part? What if my voice changed, or I grew?

Or what if they just didn't want me anymore?

"I can't wait a year," I told him. "I need to go back in. Isn't there anything you can do?"

Dr. Hamilton sighed heavily.

"Surgery is an option," he said slowly. "In fact, most doctors would tell that you that it's *the* option. But I don't think it's the right way to go in your case."

"Will I heal faster if I do it?" I asked. That was the only thing I cared about.

"Maybe?" said Dr. Hamilton. "There are no guarantees. Surgery is risky. Especially for a dancer. It could hurt more than it helps, or you could develop scar tissue that would damage your knee permanently. Or it might make everything better."

"What do *you* think we should do?" Mom asked.

"Nothing." Dr. Hamilton shrugged. "Alex is young. His knee will recover, if we let it. But that means healing on your body's timetable, not yours—and not the show's. Truthfully, Alex, you might not heal in time to return to the show. But if we perform the surgery and something goes wrong, you might not heal at all."

"We'll have to think about this," Mom said. "Get a second opinion. We have doctors back home, and—"

"Of course," said Dr. Hamilton. "Whatever you choose, I'll support you. If you decided to operate, Dr. Mung is a fantastic surgeon. For now, we'll fit Alex for a brace and get him started on a physical therapy routine to keep up his stamina and endurance."

I opened my mouth to say something, but nothing came out. What was there to say? I would heal, or I wouldn't. The show would replace me, or not. There was nothing I could do.

There was nothing I could do.

Nothing.

CHAPTER 22

Giving Back

Dear God,

It's been four weeks since my accident, and no one will talk about it. Every time I ask when I'll be better, Dr. Hamilton says it's too soon to tell. When I ask Kate when I can come back to the show, she says they don't know. I have no idea what's going on.

I'm not going to ask you for anything other than understanding. I feel so lost. I don't know what to do. I trust in you, but I'm scared.

Please help me.

When I finished saying my prayers, I slowly removed the knee brace Dr. Hamilton had given me. It extended from my hip all the way down to the top of my ankle, completely immobilizing my left leg. It was made of tough, black padding encircled by heavy metal rings. I strapped it on every morning and only took it off at night (or occasionally to scratch underneath when I couldn't resist). My leg was always itchy, hot, and inflamed. The top and bottom of the brace rubbed against my skin when I walked, creating semipermanent red rings of irritation. I felt like an impounded car with one tire locked in a boot, like I was dragging around my own personal anchor.

"Alex?" Mom called from outside my bedroom door. "You ready?"

"Yeah, come in," I said.

Then I pulled the sheet over my nose like an improvised mask.

Mom pushed the door open with her shoulder and walked inside. In her hands she cupped a bowl-shaped piece of aluminum foil. Thick tendrils of steam wafted up from it.

"Ugh," she said, her eyes watering. "Let's do this quickly."

"The faster the better," I agreed as Mom took the chair next to my bed. I peered at the thick, brown sludge inside the foil. It looked terrible, and it smelled worse. In fact, we called it "poo paste."

My cousin Emily taught us how to make it. Even once we knew for certain that I wouldn't be dancing at

Lincoln Center, she insisted on visiting.

"You're still getting the award, right?"

"Yeah, I'll be up onstage," I told her. "But I won't be dancing."

"*Pshh!* I've seen you dance before," she joked. "But I've never seen you get an award at Lincoln Center. I'm coming."

True to her word, she flew in from California a week later. When she arrived at our apartment, I couldn't help but think how much had changed since her last visit, just a month ago. Then, I'd been on top of the world, opening my first show on Broadway. Now? There were some days when I felt like I had no idea who I was. I was trapped in limbo, unable to do any of the things I used to take for granted. Aside from Dad's passing, it was the worst I'd ever felt.

I didn't even know how to be a good host. I couldn't show Emily around, not with my leg the way it was. And even though I was no longer in regular rehearsals, I still had a pretty busy schedule. They kept me in the acting sessions, to keep the script fresh in my mind. From the beginning, I went to physical therapy three times a week. I couldn't do much with my leg, but I still needed to keep up my endurance, which was important if I were ever going to return to the show. And there were stretches and delicate strengthening exercises I could do to help my knee heal properly. I spent a lot of time at PhysioArts on the arm bike, wishing I were eight blocks away, onstage at the Imperial, where I belonged. It was so close and yet so, so far.

I also used the time to bank tutoring sessions. We were required to have a certain number of hours per school year, and I figured if I could do them all while I was injured, it would make returning to the show easier—whenever *that* happened.

For the moment we'd decided to take Dr. Hamilton's advice and let my leg heal on its own. Our physician back home, Dr. Mysnyk, said that he knew Dr. Hamilton and agreed with his recommendation. Dr. Mysnyk was a family friend (his family had actually come to my opening night in *Billy*), and we trusted him completely. We scheduled a trip to Iowa so he could examine my knee himself, but until then, we decided to leave it alone and hope for the best.

If it had been anyone else visiting, I think they would have had an awful trip. But not Emily. She was always full of energy. She even helped make the Lincoln Center event fun. I was sad not to be able to do "Electricity," but it still meant a lot to accept the award, and Trent did a great job dancing. There were tons of celebrities at the event, like Tamara Tunie from *Law & Order: SVU*, and Emily helped me get photographs with all of them. I thought I'd never want to look at that award, but when we got home, I put it on the desk in my bedroom and decided it was pretty cool.

But there wasn't much to do for the rest of Emily's trip. When I told her that I couldn't really travel around, she said it didn't bother her.

"Then pull out the Wii." She smiled. "But no blaming your leg when I destroy you."

"You're on!" I laughed.

Nearly everyone in my life in New York was connected to the show, and seeing them made me feel sad and confused. But with Emily, I could just hang out and have fun. If not for her, I might seriously have become a hermit during that first month after my injury.

We barely even talked about my knee, except right when she arrived. She asked me a few questions about what I had done and how it felt, then pulled out her cell and called her mother, my auntie Polly, back in California. A few days later, a small package arrived in the mail.

"What're those?" I asked as she pulled plastic bags of dried herbs out of the package.

"A remedy," she said, "for your knee."

"Do I . . . *eat* them?" I wrinkled my nose. They didn't

smell like something I wanted to put in my mouth.

"No," Emily said. "Come to the kitchen, I'll show you."

The powders, she explained, had been sent by her mother and were a traditional Chinese herbal treatment for injuries. It was something you couldn't buy in stores, not in this country, but her family had passed down the recipe.

"Add all these powders together, mix it with vodka, and heat it on top of the stove in some foil," Emily directed me. Slowly, I hobbled around the kitchen following her instructions. "It'll form a thick paste," she continued. "That's how you know it's ready. Smear it all over your knee before you go to bed, and cover it with foil. It'll help you heal faster. Just try not to breathe while you do it. You can tell it works by how it smells."

If smell was an indicator of strength, this was definitely some powerful medicine.

Every night since, Mom and I cooked up a batch of poo paste for my leg. It really did make my knee feel better. It was warm and tingly and seemed to help with the swelling. And by this point, I would have done anything—even *eat* the poo paste—if it seemed to help. Being injured combined the two things I hated most in the world: being inactive and being unsure. And worse, they went hand in hand. The less I had to do, the more time I had to worry. It was a vicious cycle that left me staring at the ceiling every morning, having to will myself to get out of bed.

Always before, I would have tried to push through. That was my training. In gymnastics, the number one priority was performing. You focus, and you overcome. The same attitude did not prevail on Broadway.

"Absolutely not," Kate said one afternoon, when I told her I thought I could work around the pain. "You are not coming back until you are better. Do you understand?"

"I can do it," I told her. I'd done it before. "You're pregnant, and *you're* still working."

"Being pregnant and being injured are very different things," Kate said. "Also, I'm not thirteen and starring in a Broadway show three, four, five times a week. If you push and reinjure yourself, you might never heal. This is the rest of your life we're talking about."

She bent down until her head was close to mine.

"Alex, I know you don't want to hear this, but we are not risking your health to put you back in the show faster. You'll only make it worse."

I wasn't sure anything could be worse than this, but I did as Kate said. I didn't seem to have any other choice.

Thankfully, the creative team came up with an idea.

With all the buzz surrounding the show thanks to the Tony Awards, they were receiving tons of press requests every month. Some were for interviews and appearances on television shows, but many of them asked for support for charity events. They wanted a Billy to give a speech, or kick off a race, or lead a dance workshop. Because our schedules were so packed when we were in the show, we rarely had the chance to give back. Since I was out indefinitely, however, they decided to use me as a spokes-Billy.

It was the first good show-related thing to happen since my injury. In fact, I got really excited about the chance to do charity work.

My first event was just two weeks after the awards at Lincoln Center. I was asked to be a celebrity guest at the Covenant House annual Candlelight Vigil for Homeless Youth. Every year, hundreds of social workers, youth advocates, homeless and formerly homeless youth, family, friends, and supporters gathered in Times Square to bring awareness of the suffering of homeless kids. Simultaneous vigils were held in shelters, churches, and homes all around the country. I was shocked to learn that more than seventy thousand children live in Covenant House shelters across the United States, and many more were on the streets or in other homeless facilities. I couldn't imagine how hard their lives must be.

The event had a lineup of speakers from Covenant House, as well as celebrities like former New York Met Dwight "Doc" Gooden and *Guiding Light* star Karla Mosley. I had been asked to read a letter that had been left in the chapel of the Covenant House New York shelter by an unknown homeless young person.

"Just read slowly and clearly," said Juliana Hannett, the woman who facilitated all the PR done by members of *Billy Elliot*. It was her job to make sure we didn't say the wrong thing, or stumble through our lines. She was sort of like our director for press events. Because Broadway shows are always making new casting decisions, thinking about tours, and extending (or cutting short) their runs, she made sure that we didn't accidentally give out incorrect information, or say anything that wasn't ready to be public knowledge. She was also a great speaking coach and helped me overcome saying "um" whenever I was nervous.

And I was nervous tonight. As hundreds of people lit thin white candles in translucent blue holders, I practiced what I was going to say and fussed over my hair. The reading would be broadcast on the Times Square Jumbotron above my head, making me nearly fifteen feet tall and sending my voice echoing across the most famous intersection in the world.

There was a flurry of activity on the stage as the head

of Covenant House introduced me. Juliana counted down from three on her fingers, then silently cued me to walk up to the podium. As the audience applauded, I cleared my throat and began speaking.

"I feel so blessed," I said, looking out over the crowd. "I'm getting the opportunity to live out my dream on Broadway, and I believe with all my heart that every kid should have that chance."

As I said the words, I realized they were true. I *was* blessed. I *was* living out my dream. Maybe there were some bumps in the road, but was life really terrible just because I hadn't been on Broadway *long enough*? There were kids who didn't know when their next meals would be, or where they would sleep tonight. As the November wind cut across Times Square, I shivered, imagining life without my family, or where I would go tonight if we didn't have our safe, warm apartment.

I had a hard, uncertain path ahead of me, but it wasn't the end of the world—unless I let it be. Nothing is guaranteed in life. But even if I never got back into *Billy Elliot*, even if I never danced again, it didn't mean I couldn't do great things.

Getting to Broadway required a level of focus that could sometimes make it hard to see all the other possibilities in life. Reading about the struggles of this young person who had so much less than I did put my life into perspective. Maybe I was meant to be on another path, or maybe this struggle was exactly the thing I was supposed to confront and overcome in my life.

But until I had a clear sign leading me elsewhere, I was going to do everything in my power to get back on that stage.

CHAPTER 23

Father Figure

"I probably shouldn't ask you to sing now, because you're not warmed up and you don't have anybody here to play with you, but if you wanted to do a little something . . ."

Rosie O'Donnell looked at Trent and me while Misty, her long-haired Chihuahua, trembled in her lap. I could barely believe I was actually at her house, sitting on her couch, being interviewed for her radio show. And now she was asking me to sing with her.

Trent and I looked at each other and shrugged. This wasn't part of the interview plan, but Juliana was giving us a big smile from the control room, so I guessed it was our choice.

"Sure," Trent and I said simultaneously.

And next thing I knew, we were singing "Electricity"

on air with Rosie!

At this point, I'd been out of the show for nearly three months. I'd been looked at by Dr. Hamilton and Dr. Mysnyk, taken MRIs and X-rays, gone to physical therapy weekly, and smeared poo paste on my leg nightly. And my knee was finally beginning to improve. Not much, and not fast, but it was a little stronger, and every day at PhysioArts I could bend it a little more.

Still, the show had no idea when—or if—I would return. The silence was driving us crazy. All Mom wanted was an answer. Would I go back? Would I be paid for the weeks I was out? Would I go on disability? Not only could the show not answer us, they couldn't even tell us *when* they would be able to answer us.

Luckily, my body seemed in no hurry to grow. I was still the shortest of the Billys, and my voice hadn't changed. So long as my knee continued to improve, I was optimistic I would return . . . eventually.

In the meantime, I kept doing press and charity events. In November, I kicked off the Kids Fun Run at the inaugural Damon Runyon 5K Race for Cancer Research with the New York Yankees. Working with a cancer charity made me feel good, even better, in some ways, than working with Covenant House. It felt like I was doing something on Dad's behalf, and I knew he'd be proud.

In December, Liam and I appeared on *Good Morning America* to donate to their coat drive for the homeless. That night, Liam performed as Billy for the first time. It was bittersweet. I was excited for him, but I couldn't help but wish I were up there. I'd been Billy exactly four times, which was more than I'd ever expected, and so much less than I had come to hope.

It would have been easy for the show to cut their losses, bring on new Billys, and see if I still fit the part after I healed. Instead, the public relations people put me forward as the face of the show. Friends would send photos of me on billboards and taxis they ran into around the country. It shocked me every time. It was the show's way of keeping me involved and letting me know they were committed to bringing me back. It also made practical sense, as I had much more free time than all the other Billys.

Today, Trent and I were on *Rosie Radio*, Rosie O'Donnell's SiriusXM radio show. It was the most laid-back press event I'd done yet. Rosie lived just an hour outside the city, and she actually ran her radio show out of her house. Or well, one of her houses. Rosie owned a small cluster of normal-looking homes on a pretty cul-de-sac, out of which she raised her family and ran her businesses. We entered one through the kitchen and walked upstairs to a converted radio studio. A dividing wall with a large soundproof window separated the control room from the studio itself, where Rosie, Trent, Misty, and I sat on the couch and chatted. Rosie was such a natural host that I felt completely comfortable and often forgot we were live. The half-hour interview went by like nothing. We were saying our on-air good-byes when Rosie made one final announcement.

"We have a Wii and all the games, and we're delivering it tonight to the theater!" She smiled as Trent and I stared in shock.

"Thank you!" we rushed to say.

She was so nice, we didn't have the heart to tell her we weren't allowed to have a TV in our dressing room—too noisy. Since I already had a Wii, I let Trent have it, while I took the games. It was such a sweet, generous gesture on Rosie's part, and it reinforced everything I had come to learn about celebrities in my time at *Billy Elliot*: they were all really nice. Maybe it was just the ones who participated in charity events, or went out of their way to talk to a kid who was (until recently) completely unknown, but nearly every famous person I met was incredibly kind to me.

At the end of January, *Billy Elliot* celebrated its five hundredth performance on Broadway with a sold-out house. In fact, even *I* had to stand at the back in order to get in. Seeing the show again reminded me just how much I loved it. When Billy sets off for ballet school in London at the end, I couldn't help but tear up. Part of me wanted to warn him that going to the city wasn't always the incredible journey you hoped it would be. But maybe that's the beauty of the show: it promises nothing except for the *possibility* of a happy ending—much like life.

Afterward, the entire cast and crew headed over to Glass House Tavern, a restaurant not far from the theater. Company management had rented the entire upstairs for the after-party. It was an elegant space with big stone chimneys and dark heavy wood tables. Counting me, there were five Billys in attendance. Now that I wasn't on the regular rehearsal schedule, I didn't see much of them outside of tutoring. Liam and I would play video games occasionally, and I got lunch with Trent sometimes. But most of us Billys kept to ourselves. Sometimes it could get weird playing the same role. By some unspoken rule we never talked about who was performing at what show or press event or awards ceremony. It was the only way we could be friends, by letting management assign us when and where they wanted, and not competing among ourselves for shows.

"Alex!" Stephen yelled as I entered Glass House. "Come check it out."

He waved me over to a table by the wall, where a giant sheet cake was decorated with an icing version of the *Billy Elliot* logo, complete with a leaping silhouette of Billy. Underneath, it said 500TH PERFORMANCE. I have a big sweet tooth, and it looked delicious. I hurried over to get a bite.

"Dayton! Michael! Trent! Liam!" Stephen called all the other Billys over. "Come on, come on. Tonight's your night. All of you."

Even though I hadn't performed in months, Stephen treated me no differently from any of the other Billys. As we all gathered around the cake, flashes popped left and right. Being actors, we couldn't help but pose. For a few minutes, we played at being celebrities and pretended our friends and family were eager paparazzi. Eventually, Stephen quieted the room.

"I just want to say a few words to congratulate these fine actors on the fantastic job they have done, five hundred times in a row!" Stephen said, smiling at all five of us. "But first . . ."

He motioned for us to gather closer. We jostled in, and I ended up standing directly to his right. Suddenly I felt his hand on the back of my head. Before I could say a word, he pushed my face into the cake!

Icing and yellow cake flew everywhere. I could feel the frosting squirt up my nose. The entire room burst into shocked laughter, and even though I couldn't really breathe, I joined in.

I'll give them something to laugh about, I thought as I stood up straight and smiled big, crumbs falling from my chin.

"Sorry, Alex, I couldn't resist," said Stephen as he came over with a napkin to wipe my face clean. I waited until he was only a few inches away.

"Me either," I told him.

Stephen looked confused for a second, but before he figured it out, I pushed him into the remains of the cake. Now there definitely wasn't any to eat, but I have to say it was worth it. A cake war lasted just long enough for Liam to end up splattered with icing as well, before waiters rushed over to deal with the mess.

Even though I tried to clean up at the restaurant, I found stray locks of hair cemented together with icing when I got ready for bed that night, and crumbs plastered to my shoulders the next morning.

"Dad," I said, before falling asleep. "Thank you for sending me someone to look out for me. Everything's still up in the air, but between you, Mom, and Stephen,

I'm feeling hopeful again. Something's going to change, I know it."

Two weeks later, Kate called to tell me it was time to rejoin rehearsals.

CHAPTER 24

My Return

"I don't know," Dr. Hamilton said as he stared at my X-rays. He scratched his head and *tsk*-ed his tongue. I sat on the edge of my seat, silently begging.

I'd been back in rehearsals for a month now, slowly getting up to speed. We'd had to change some of my routines to accommodate my leg, but not as many as I had feared. I was absolutely forbidden to do any big acrobatics, so my entire "Electricity" number had to be rechoreographed. And even though I'd kept up my endurance by doing endless hours of cardio, my legs still needed strengthening. But it didn't take long before I could do the full show without any hiccups.

"Wear this," the therapist at PhysioArts said before the first dance rehearsal of my return. She handed me a brace that had a horseshoe-shaped piece of padding threaded into it. “This should keep your knee from ever touching the ground, even if you’re kneeling.”

“Thanks,” I said. “How long do I have to wear it for?”

“From now on,” she said. “We’re not taking any chances. And there’s no more running in the mezzanine, or doing any warm-ups on a hard floor anywhere in the theater.”

Everyone was walking on eggshells when it came to my leg, which I guess made sense, because it was a serious injury. But I was nearly recovered, and I’d dealt with so many accidents before, I almost didn’t understand the issue. I’d hurt it, it was better, and now it was time for me to come back. I was sick of waiting.

There was one last hurdle to jump through. I needed a doctor to sign me back in. If Dr. Hamilton agreed, March 14, 2010—five months *to the day* after my injury—would be my first day back as Billy Elliot.

I wanted it badly, and not just because I was desperate to get back into the show. That performance was actually a fund-raiser for Hancher Auditorium at the University of Iowa. Nearly seventy-five Iowans had purchased tickets, and though they didn’t know me, they were coming in part to see the local boy who had made it big. I didn’t want to disappoint them. But it wasn’t up to me.

Please, I pleaded silently as Dr. Hamilton stared at my X-rays.

"Okay," he said finally. "I'll sign you in."

"Thank you!" I wanted to leap over his desk and hug him.

"But you need to be careful. I don't want you back in here in four weeks because you pushed too hard and tore it again. It could very easily return."

He looked me square in the eye.

"You were lucky this time, got it?"

"Yes, sir." I nodded. "I promise I won't do anything stupid."

And I meant it.

At least, I did when I said it. . . .

My first show back went as smoothly as it could. The Iowans in the audience cheered at everything I did, and although I was hyperaware of the changes we'd made to accommodate my leg, no one else seemed to notice.

Being back felt like a dream come true. No more sitting around, no more physical therapy, and no more wondering what was going to happen to me. Finally, all the obstacles were gone, and I could do what I had come here to do: perform on Broadway, dance my heart out, and make Dad (and Mom) proud.

But I couldn't stop thinking about the parts we'd cut, and wishing I could do the full thing. Maybe it's the perfectionist in me, but I hate doing less than I know I'm capable of. But I knew if there was even the slightest chance I'd reinjure myself, they'd pull me right out—even if we were only halfway through the show! About once every other month, a Billy had to be removed at intermission, usually because he'd had a minor injury or gotten sick. Thankfully, there was always a backup Billy on-site, waiting in the dressing room, but I still didn't want it to happen to me. So I played it safe . . . mostly.

But just two weeks after I returned to the show, Kenny Ortega was coming to see me. He was the man who choreographed *Dirty Dancing*, and he directed and choreographed the *High School Musical* franchise. In other words, he was a very big deal. We'd met a few times in the past—he had actually started to become friends with our family over the past couple of years. But now he was coming to see me and I wanted to impress him.

Stephen had been urging me not to pursue a career in dance. He said I should keep up with ballet, but focus on my education or something else that didn't have such a short life span. Dancers were prone to injury, as I'd already learned, and even without accidents to cut their careers short, most were finished by their thirties. I knew Stephen was right, but impressing Kenny Ortega was important to me. He'd flown all this way to see me back in the show. Even if I didn't want to dance forever, I wanted to dance my best right now!

As I warmed up before the show, I tested my knee. It twinged a little, but no more than it did after a normal workout.

I'm fine, I thought. *I'll do the real thing, just this once, then I'll go back to the new version Kate choreographed.*

"Got anything for Dollar Friday?" asked one of the stagehands, pulling me out of my worries. He had a huge jar filled with ones and fives. Every Friday, anyone who wanted could put a bill in with their name on it. At the end of the show, a winner was drawn and received the whole pot. I liked playing—it was one of those things that made the show seem like a family. But not tonight.

"Sorry," I said, patting my costume. "No real pockets."

And besides, I had enough to worry about tonight. I took some aspirin as a precaution to help with the swelling, and made sure my new brace was on as tightly as possible. I performed most of the show as expected, and when Act I finished, I felt fine. I knew, without a doubt, that I could pull off my acrobatics tonight. But I also knew I was going to be in trouble if I did. I watched the monitors during intermission, checking out the audience and trying to spot Kenny, but I couldn't see him. I was nervous about Act II, because that's when Billy's really big number happens, "Electricity." It had been five and a half months since the last time I'd done the gymnastics routine full out, and I hadn't even tried an aerial cartwheel since. What if I didn't hit my tricks? What if I fell? What if I embarrassed *and* reinjured myself? That would be the worst-case scenario.

As we came closer and closer to "Electricity," I ran through the routine in my head. I kept coming to the same conclusion: I could do it. I could do the whole thing. I could do a back layout and an aerial cartwheel, and I could probably hit the landing.

As the music to "Electricity" began to swell, the woman playing the judge from the ballet school asked me (as Billy) what it felt like when I danced. I shot a final look at the audience. The house was full and Kenny was out there. I *had* to do it. I had to show him what it felt like when *I* danced.

I put all of my heart into "Electricity" that night, because I knew I had to make up in enthusiasm and energy for what I was missing in practice and endurance. As the music built to a crescendo, I prayed.

Please let this work.

Then I hit the floor.

Cartwheel, handspring, back handspring, backflip—I hit every single trick, including the back layout and aerial cartwheel and stuck the landings. The crowd went wild. The front row jumped to their feet. The applause was deafening. And best of all, I was winded, but my knee felt fine. All those hours at PhysioArts had paid off.

As I stepped offstage to change for my next scene, I knew I was in trouble.

"You. Me. Afterward," said Tom, who was filling in for Kate that night.

He looked furious.

My stomach dropped. Surely, once I explained, he would understand, I rationalized, and I would call Kate and explain to her too. But I knew she was going to be mad regardless.

Kenny Ortega came backstage as soon as the show ended.

"Alex!" he said, grabbing me into a hug. "That was fantastic. Really, fantastic."

"Thank you," I replied. "That means a lot, coming from you."

"I can't stay long—and it's probably past your bedtime anyway. But next time I'm in New York, why don't you, your mom, and I all get dinner?"

"We'd love to!"

"Great," Kenny said. "And tell your mom hi for me!"

When I saw Kate the next day, her voice was cold and stony. "You risked your health to impress Kenny Ortega."

When she put it that way, it sounded much less reasonable than it had in my head.

"Kate, I'm sorry. I really am. But I knew—"

"No," Kate said. "You didn't *know*. You can't *know*. What if you had slipped? What if someone left a prop in the wrong place, and you tripped over it? What if your knee re-tore? Do you know how many promising careers I've seen destroyed by tricks like the one you pulled last night?"

"I know, but . . . that didn't happen. It worked out fine."

My excuse sounded thin, even to me.

"Alex, you are fourteen years old. A serious injury now won't just end your career. It could stop you from growing properly."

Kate paused and ran one hand through her hair. In that moment I saw all the fear and worry that were behind the anger. Guilt struck me like a slap across the face. Kate was trying to protect me. I felt ungrateful and childish.

"I'm sorry, Kate." I wished I could sink into the floor and disappear. "I promise you, this won't happen again."

"I know it won't," she said. "Because if it does, and you reinjure yourself, you're out of the show. If you cannot, or will not, take care of yourself, we will do it for you."

"I'm really sorry, Kate. I didn't think about what I was doing, and I won't do it again."

I felt like I was going to cry. I'd let down someone who trusted me, and I'd put my own health in danger. This wasn't the kind of person I'd promised Dad I would become.

Kate hugged me.

"You know I'm only mad because I'm worried for you?" she said.

"I know." I tried not to sniffle.

"Good. Never do this again. See you tomorrow."

With that, Kate left. I sat in my dressing room for another minute, thinking about the previous night. What I had done was stupid and careless, and I was lucky to get off as lightly as I had. From now on, I swore to myself, my health would come first.

Besides, Kate was right. I could do permanent damage to my body. If I handled it right, *Billy Elliot* would be just the beginning of my career. In more ways than one, I needed to start thinking about what I was doing next. There was no way this job was permanent. If I didn't injure myself, I'd age out, or the show would close. I had to start planning ahead.

But for the moment I was back, and I was ready to finally enjoy my life as a Broadway star. True to his word, Kenny Ortega returned to New York frequently, and he took me out nearly every time. The funny thing about meeting celebrities is that it never happened the way I would expect. It was always offhand, accidental, and nonchalant, like the time I spoke to Jennifer Grey.

Kenny, Mom, and I were at Joe Allen splitting nachos and guacamole and talking about life in New York. I was telling them about my thoughts about my life after *Billy*, how I wanted to continue studying ballet while I applied to college, when suddenly Kenny's phone rang.

"Sorry," he said, looking at the number. "Gotta take this. Jennifer! Hey! Great to hear from you."

He paused just long enough to snag a nacho from the tray.

"I'm having dinner with some friends. Actually, you should talk to one of them. This is Alex. He's a dancer, and he's on Broadway right now."

He put his hand over the mouthpiece.

"Jennifer Grey," he mouthed. "From *Dirty Dancing*."

As though I didn't know who Jennifer Grey was! I might not have been born in the eighties, but I don't think there's a dancer alive who hasn't seen that movie.

"She wants some advice," Kenny said, thrusting his cell at me. "Help her out."

With no other choice, I took the phone.

"Hi?" I said, unsure what useful advice I could possibly give Jennifer Grey.

"Alex, I'm Jennifer," she said sweetly. "Great to meet you. Kenny says you're a dancer?"

"Ballet, mostly," I told her. "But I'm on Broadway right now. In *Billy Elliot*."

"So cool!" she said excitedly. "Congratulations. You're just the person I need."

"Really?" I said, confused. "How can I help you?"

"I'm on *Dancing with the Stars* right now, and it's been a long time since I've danced this much. What do you eat to keep your energy up? It's so tiring!"

"Well," I said, shocked that she'd actually asked a question I could help with, "I usually have a Clif Bar and a banana at intermission. That's my power snack."

"Cool," she said. It sounded like she was taking notes. "And how do you warm up?"

"Jumping jacks, running . . . a little bit of everything

really. I just try to do stuff that'll loosen me up." I thought for a second, and something occurred to me. "Don't do it on concrete, though. You could injure yourself. Watch out for your knees."

"Awesome," she said. "Do you watch *Dancing with the Stars*?"

"I will now," I told her, and we laughed.

"Well, wish me luck if you do. Say good-bye to Kenny for me—I'll let you get back to dinner."

With a click, she was gone.

"Kid's a natural," Kenny said to Mom as I stared at the phone. Had I really just given advice to Jennifer Grey? Talk about worlds being flipped upside down.

"Was she nice?" Mom asked.

"Really nice," I mumbled. "I just can't believe . . . I mean, why would she want my advice? I'm just a kid."

"Alex," Kenny said, shaking his head in shock. "You're on Broadway! No, strike that, you're in a *title role* on Broadway. You haven't been 'just a kid' in a while. And this is only the beginning. Mark my words, you won't believe the places you'll go."

As we finished lunch, I thought about what Kenny had said. I guess maybe I wasn't the same kid I thought I was anymore. Even though all of this seemed so new, it was my reality now, and I needed to get used to it. But

I didn't think Kenny was totally right. I mean, what could possibly top being on Broadway, meeting Rosie O'Donnell, *and* talking to Jennifer Grcy?

As it happened, I was about to find out.

CHAPTER 25

Inspired

"Please take off your shoes, belts, anything metal in your pockets, any jewelry, portable phones, etc., and put them in the bin before you pass through the metal detector. Thank you."

The guard repeated his speech in a monotone every few minutes. I'd been waiting for nearly an hour, so I'd heard it enough times that I could recite it from memory. A long line of would-be guests snaked down the hall from the guard station, patiently waiting and playing with their cell phones. Finally it was my turn.

"Alex Ko?" The guard looked up from a list of names on his computer.

"Yes." I nodded.

"Birth certificate?"

I passed him the thin piece of paper, which we'd

ordered from Iowa just for this reason. He stared at it intently before running a black light over it to look for forgeries. I must have checked out, because he waved me through the metal detector and handed me a dark blue identification badge with the letter *A* on it.

"Wear this at all times," he said without looking up. "Liam Redhead?" he called out next.

"Wow," I whispered to myself as I gazed past the security checkpoint down the long and lavish hallway. The White House looks great in pictures, but you have to be there to get the full effect.

Liam and I, along with Dayton Tavares and Jacob Clemente, two other Billys, had flown to D.C. to lead a workshop for the inaugural session of the White House Dance Series, a new initiative that the first lady had begun as part of her health and fitness drive. I'd been back in the show for a few months now, and I was at the peak of my time as Billy. Being invited to the White House was both an honor and a privilege. We would be onstage beside members of the New York City Ballet, the Alvin Ailey American Dance Theater, and the Washington Ballet—not to mention the first lady herself, Michelle Obama. The event combined performances, a tribute to choreographer Judith Jamison (the artistic director of Alvin Ailey), and a dance workshop for nearly one hundred young people from around the country. It was an afternoon event taking place in the East Room, an elegant ballroom with three giant crystal chandeliers, a beautiful parquet floor, and stately portraits of past presidents hanging on the walls.

Or at least, that's where the event was *going* to take place. But even though it took forever to get through security, we still arrived really early. The East Room wasn't even set up when we walked in. Juliana told us to settle down and wait, then went across the room to talk to the organizers of the event.

"Hey, Alex, look!" said Liam as we explored the empty ballroom. "Over there—isn't that where the president makes all his speeches?"

I went down the hallway, where some workers were setting up a podium and chairs. It looked like they were getting ready for a big press event. Later, we found out that President Obama was making a televised announcement that evening, but at the time we weren't sure what was going on.

"Maybe? It's hard to tell. Everything here looks so . . . *presidential*," I said. "Like you expect to turn a corner and run into him at any moment."

"I know," said Liam. "Look, the workers are gone."

The podium was sitting there, lit up and alone, graced with the presidential seal.

"Wanna take a picture?" Liam asked. "I'll take yours if you take mine."

"Sure!" I smiled. I looked around to tell Juliana, but she was busy on the other side of the room, now talking to security.

We'll be quick, I thought. *No point in worrying her.*

Liam and I slipped out of the East Room and into the empty hallway. No alarms went off, and I didn't see any SWAT teams running our way, so I figured we were safe. I looked around. Liam was right: this was definitely where President Obama gave his speeches. I'd seen him on TV, in this very spot, dozens of times. I crept up behind the podium and imagined myself giving an important address. I couldn't believe I was *literally* standing in President Obama's footsteps.

"Okay, pose," Liam said as he jogged away from me. "Ready? Three, two . . . one . . . Go!"

I threw my left leg high behind me and extended my arms above my head in an arabesque. I couldn't imagine a more appropriate pose for a photo at the White House.

An arabesque is one of the most regal poses in any kind of dance.

"Your turn," I said to Liam. We switched positions and Liam did an arabesque of his own. We traded places a few more times, each of us trying to get the most reach, the most extension, the most perfect arabesque we could do, because this was a once-in-a-lifetime opportunity.

"That's your new Facebook profile pic right there," I said to Liam as I showed him the photos I'd taken on my phone.

"Awesome." He slapped me five. "Now what?"

We both looked back the way we'd come. No one seemed to have noticed we were gone. Through the open door, I could see Juliana still talking to the guards.

"We should go back in," I said. "They'll miss us soon."

"Yeah," Liam agreed.

Neither of us moved.

"I mean, we don't have anything to do for another hour," I said.

"And if we went back in, we'd probably just be in the way," Liam added.

"And who knows if we'll ever visit here again. . . ." I trailed off.

We both looked longingly down the hall. Who wanted to be cooped up in the East Room, when we could actually get to see the place where everything happened? This was the center of American democracy. *Lincoln* had walked these floors. It was almost our patriotic duty to go exploring.

"Come on," Liam said decisively. We snuck past the

podium and took a left at the first intersection. The hallway we entered was empty, but there were footsteps coming from behind us. We walked away from them as fast as we could without running. Doors opened onto the hall at random intervals, but all of them were closed, and we were afraid to open them. The last thing we wanted was to surprise a group of armed Secret Service agents.

"Duh-duh-da-da-da-dadaduh." I quietly sang the *Mission: Impossible* theme song as we moved quickly down the hall. The footsteps behind us were getting closer.

"Here!" Liam said, pulling me into the first open door we found. Inside was the smallest room I saw that day in the White House. It wasn't much bigger than our living room at home—and it already had people in it. My heart jumped into my throat. Was it a crime to wander the White House unescorted? I wondered. I was about to find out.

"Excuse me," said the large security guard standing by the door. "Can I see your IDs, please?"

"Is that Bo?" Liam asked, ignoring the security guard entirely and addressing the young man with a black fluffy dog on a leash. I held up my blue ID tag at the guard and hoped for the best.

"Yes," the dog walker said. "But you're not supposed

to be in here. Aren't you with the dance program?"

"We're from *Billy Elliot*," I said, partly to the walker and partly to the guard, who was giving Liam an angry look. "But I really wanted to meet Bo."

It wasn't a lie, not entirely. I love dogs, and I really *did* want to meet Bo.

"Can I pet him?" I said.

"No," the dog walker replied. "Really, no one's supposed to touch him."

Bo looked up at us, his intelligent eyes begging us to stroke his fluffy head. He was a Portuguese water dog, and looked exactly like a curly-haired stuffed animal. How could we resist?

"Please?" said Liam.

The man looked around quickly, but we were alone aside from the security guard, who seemed bored now that it was clear we weren't pint-size spies.

"All right," the walker said. "But just once."

I'm happy to report that Bo Obama is a great first dog: cute, smart, friendly, and very, very fluffy. I wish I could have gotten a picture with him, but even petting him seemed to make his handler nervous. I wanted to get out before he made the security guard escort us back to the East Room.

"Thanks!" I said over my shoulder as I pulled Liam

away from the dog and out of the room. "Where to now?" I whispered.

Liam shrugged. The dance program would be starting soon. I almost suggested we head back when I spotted another open door.

"Let's just look," I said. I darted down the hall and peeked my head in.

The room had two big, heavy red armchairs sitting atop a thick Oriental rug. There were a couple of ornate wooden desks and armoires, as well as the antique paintings that seemed to be required decor for every room in the White House. I guess after forty-four presidents and first families, you end up with a lot of portraits. But what caught my eye was an open cabinet built into one wall. I couldn't tell what was inside it, exactly, but it looked like thin sheets of metal stacked vertically.

"Whoa . . . cool. What is *that*?" I wondered.

"I don't know," Liam said as he poked his head in next to mine. "But I know how to find out!"

Quick as a flash, Liam was in the room and tugging on one of the sheets.

"Careful!" I whispered as I ran over to help him. Slowly, we tugged it out of the cabinet to reveal a giant map of Asia that was intricately detailed. When fully unrolled, it hung in front of the cabinet with a little stand to keep it in place. It was metal only on the outer edge—the rest was a sort of heavy canvas.

"Cool," said Liam. "The president has the best toys."

"It's one of the perks of being president," I agreed. "Like Air Force One and the right to skip every line at Disneyland."

There were dozens of other maps in the cabinet, and I wanted to pull each one out and examine it. I could just picture the president meeting foreign ambassadors in this room to discuss trade agreements and national security issues. I shivered. I couldn't believe how awesome my life had become. I, Alex Ko from Iowa City, was an invited guest at the White House, exploring the president's stuff. For the first time, I actually felt famous.

"What do you think's in there?" Liam asked, pointing to the only other door in the Map Room.

I shrugged and went to open it.

"Sweet," I said. Liam started to run over.

"Hold up!" I yelled as I slipped into the room and closed the door behind me. "It's just the bathroom."

I'd needed one for a while. After I washed my hands, I checked the time on my phone. It was after noon, and the workshop was starting soon. It was time for Liam and me to head back. But as I wiped my hands, I noticed something strange about the paper towels: they had the

White House seal emblazoned on them. I took a few as souvenirs.

"Catch," I said as I stepped out of the room and lobbed a pile of towels at Liam.

"Ew!" he said. "What did you do that for?"

"Souvenir," I told him. "Look at them. Closely."

I slipped more into my bag as Liam started laughing.

"Awesome! Thanks, Alex."

"No problem," I said. "But we should get back."

"Think they've noticed we're missing?"

"If Juliana had noticed, I don't think we'd be missing anymore," I replied. I was surprised we'd managed to stay free for this long. Management was usually pretty strict at events like this, but we'd gotten lucky. When we slipped back into the East Room, it was clear that no one had even noticed we were gone. If it hadn't been for the paper towels in my bag (which I still have, to this day, as a souvenir on my bookshelf), it all might never have happened.

"Alex, Liam, Dayton, Jacob!" Juliana called our names from the other side of the East Room. "We're going to get started soon, but first there's someone who wants to meet you."

Juliana led us into the hallway. Right away, I noticed that the farther we went, the more security there was. I felt a tingle of expectation run down my spine. This could mean only one thing. . . .

Finally, we reached a door guarded by four Secret Service agents. There were other dancers already waiting. We joined them in line, and security ushered us in. There, in the center of the room, was the first lady, Michelle Obama!

"Welcome," she said as we entered.

My jaw dropped. I couldn't believe I was meeting the first lady of the United States of America. I also couldn't believe how *tall* she was. I mean, she had to be at least six feet. At least. And that wasn't counting her shoes.

"Remember," Juliana whispered, "don't say anything unless she talks to you first."

The guards kept us in line, and one by one, the first lady shook hands with us. As she came closer to me, my heart started pounding. I'd been nervous about meeting famous people before, but never like this. Celebrities do cool things like star in movies and write books, but the first lady actually helped decide how our entire country was run. Hers was a whole new level of power and fame, and I couldn't believe that I was actually meeting her. Soon she was three people away in line. Then two. Then there was just one person between the first lady and me.

Then she turned to take my hand.

"Oh my gosh, you're tall," I blurted out.

"Alex!" Juliana shushed me, embarrassed.

I couldn't believe what I'd just said. I clapped my hand over my mouth.

Luckily, the first lady laughed.

"Thank you," she said. "It's the heels." She winked at me, shook my hand, and moved down the line.

Soon after that, the workshop started and I found myself leading a hundred kids through "Solidarity," a big ballet number that intercuts scenes of Billy in dance class with his father and brother fighting armed guards at the mines. I felt doubly blessed. I was both giving back to the community and meeting some of my heroes at the same time. I could barely believe my luck.

After the lesson, a tiny girl in tights came up to me, her black ponytail shaking with nerves.

"Excuse me?" she said, in a voice just one step above a whisper.

"Hi there," I said, shaking her hand. "I'm Alex. Did you enjoy the workshop?"

"Yes," she said. "I know you. I mean, I saw you on Broadway. Can . . . can . . . can I have your autograph?" Shyly, she held out a pen and notepad.

"*My* autograph?" I asked, surprised. "Sure, of course."

I was in a room with Michelle Obama, Judith

Jamison, and at least a dozen other famous dancers, and this girl was asking for *my* autograph. Kenny's words about the places I would go came back to me then, and I realized he was right. I wanted to tell each of these kids to keep dancing, keep trying, because you never knew where life would take you. In fact, I wanted to ask this girl for *her* autograph, because if I could come from Iowa City and end up leading a workshop at the White House, who knew where *she* would go. Maybe one day *I'd* be watching *her* dance, or taking a workshop from her, or shaking her hand as the first lady of America.

Or as the president.

If there is anything that being Billy taught me about life it's this: you never know what will happen next. Chance leads to coincidence, which breeds opportunity, and allows for victory. A loss precedes a gain, failure creates room for success. At some point, every single one of us in the White House was just a child, dreaming big. Like me. Like Billy. Like the little girl.

"I'm going to be up on that stage someday," she said, after I signed her notepad. The look of determination on her face was one I knew well. I'd seen it in the mirror every day my whole life.

"Keep dreaming," I told her, "and you will."

CHAPTER 26

The Hard Side of Celebrity

After I got home from the White House, I raced to post the photos Liam and I had taken. Because my family and friends were so spread out, I was a huge Facebook user. I loved seeing what my teachers in Iowa were up to and reading comments from my family in California and Las Vegas. But now that I'd been in *Billy Elliot* for a while, I was getting more and more friend requests from people I didn't know. I felt weird rejecting them, because they were all so nice. But it was also strange to accept their requests, because I didn't know any of them.

At first, I said yes to everyone. They were reaching out in kindness, and I wanted to do the same. But it wasn't long before things got . . . *weird.* Most of the fans I met on Facebook were wonderful people doing amazing things with their lives, and I loved hearing their thoughts on the show. Some of them, however, had a hard time telling the difference between seeing me in *Billy Elliot* and being my friend in real life. Maybe they were lonely, or confused, or sick, I don't know. I think it's part of our obsession with famous people. We get so used to being able to read about them in magazines, or see photos, that fans come to expect things, and can get upset when those expectations aren't met. And some of them take it too far.

The first comment on my White House photos appeared only a few seconds after I posted them. It was from a man I'd never met, who lived in New York and had seen the show at least a dozen times. I know because he messaged me after every performance he attended.

Great photos!!!!!! he wrote. *Coming 2 my party this wknd???? U never answered my invite.*

My stomach flip-flopped. He'd been inviting me to parties, shows, and other events for weeks. Each time, I felt more uncomfortable. At first, they'd just been mass Facebook invites, but when I ignored those, he sent me individual messages. When I didn't respond to the messages, he started posting on my wall. Now he was commenting on everything I did, demanding a response.

Who is this guy? I thought. He made me feel really weird, and he wasn't the only one. Another fan had taken photos of me onstage and sent them, anonymously, to Mom at her job. The photos were pretty and maybe he meant it as a nice gesture, but it made me feel watched. A third guy had posted that I was his "real son" and he was going to "come get me." It was probably a joke, but it wasn't one I was comfortable with. But at least those guys commented and disappeared. This guy kept coming back, and each time he was more insistent.

"Mom?" I called out to the other room. "Will you look at something?"

"What is it, Alex?" she asked.

"This Facebook stuff. I don't know, it's making me feel weird. Read this."

I showed Mom the comments and messages. She read them in silence, but I could tell from her furrowed forehead that she was upset.

"Alex, you should have shown me this before," she said. "This is not okay. I don't you want to talk to him anymore."

"I never have," I told her. "He just keeps messaging me."

"Then you should block him, sweetie," Mom said, scrolling through all his invitations. "I don't like this one bit."

That was exactly what I was hoping she would say. A few clicks of the mouse later and he was out of my life forever.

Or so I thought. . . .

After the end of the show the next night, I left the theater by the stage door, as usual. There were always a few dozen audience members camped outside waiting for autographs. I loved meeting fans and signing their Playbills. It was one of my favorite parts of being in the show. But that night I didn't get to sign a single one.

At the front of the line was a large man with a scowl on his face. As soon as I left the stage door, he started calling my name.

"Alex!" he said loudly. "Alex! Why'd you block me? I just want to be your friend, man. What gives?"

My heart stopped. This was the creeper from Facebook. I didn't know what to do.

"I . . . I didn't block you," I stammered. There was just a thin rope separating us, and even though there was a security guard nearby, I could easily imagine this guy leaping right over it. My guardian had stepped back inside, but he had already called a cab and I could see it idling across the street. There was a long line of people waiting to meet me, but I couldn't stay, not with this guy here.

"I'm not on Facebook much," I lied. "In fact, I'm deleting it. I didn't block you. I have to go!" I yelled over my shoulder as I raced into the cab. My heart didn't stop pounding until the door was locked behind me and the taxi was gliding into traffic on Eighth Avenue. That night, I deleted my Facebook profile and began to understand the hard parts of being a celebrity.

Hands down, I can't imagine a better job than being in *Billy Elliot*. But there were problems too, and the longer I was in the show, the more apparent they became.

The biggest one was the most difficult to do anything about. I was performing three or four times a week. Even though I was in near-peak condition, that kind of repetitive stress takes a physical toll. I developed a long list of minor injuries, starting with my knees. Dr. Hamilton had been right: I had Osgood-Schlatter disease, and no matter how much stretching and strengthening I did, there were nights when the repetition of the same moves over and over again was too much for me. I'd learned my lesson, and there was no more trying to push through, but that meant I had to miss more performances.

But even worse than the physical stuff was the mental monotony. When I wasn't in the show, I was rehearsing it, or talking about it in an interview, or doing a scene from it for a charity event. Technically, I was with the Broadway company longer than any other Billy. For two years, everything I did in life revolved around the same three hours of singing and dancing. Back in Iowa, if anyone had told me the day would come when I found being on Broadway at all boring or routine, I'd have laughed. But after a while, even the best music in the world starts to sound repetitive. There were times when I felt like I was in that Bill Murray movie *Groundhog Day*, living the same day over and over again on a loop. I looked for ways to make the show feel new again, because I knew if I lost interest, I'd never give the audience the fully committed performance they deserved. I had to find a solution, so I called Stephen, which recently I'd been doing more and more often. The closer the end of my time in the show came, the more Stephen came to be a support figure for me.

When I was first injured, Mom and I were frustrated that he never sat us down and told us what would happen to me. But as the weeks went on, we realized there was no way he could do this. There was no time line for my knee, and though the show was doing well, you never knew when things might change. In fact, all the principal contracts had to be re-signed every six months, which is pretty standard on Broadway.

Now he was already working on his next project, the film adaptation of the best-selling book *Extremely Loud & Incredibly Close*, and Billy Elliot was going strong—on Broadway and elsewhere. To date, the show had toured twice, and had productions in New York, London, Sydney, Chicago, Toronto, and Seoul. It was impossible to expect Stephen to pay personal attention to me, one Billy from one of many productions.

And yet somehow he did. Not long after the White House event, Mom called me one afternoon during tutoring.

"Stephen just called," she said.

"Is someone sick?" I asked. "Does he need me to go on tomorrow?"

"He wants to get dinner," she continued.

"Tonight? I'll be home in a few hours."

"No," Mom said. "I mean, he was actually asking *me* for a meeting. I think he wants to check up on you."

That unexpected call was the beginning of a close friendship between Stephen and our family. He didn't just make time to deal with me, as part of the show, he made time to interact with me as a person, to get to know Mom, Matt, and John, and to look out for us. We didn't see him a lot, because he was rarely in New

York, and when he was, he was there on business. But from then on, we knew beyond a shadow of a doubt that he would do what he could for us. There were still no guarantees, but it helped quiet the feeling of panic I had inside me. It also meant that we could turn to him with questions. As I began to explore what I would do next, Stephen became my guide. So when I felt I was starting to age out of the show, he was the first person I turned to.

Thankfully, he had dealt with this issue before.

"You're getting older now, Alex," he told me one evening after he'd seen a random performance. "We should change the way you do some of the scenes. I'm going to have you work with Mark on aging up the part."

I thought Mark Schneider, the new resident director, would just give me new directions, but instead, he helped me figure out what it meant to portray Billy as a twelve- or thirteen-year-old instead of an eleven-year-old. It was this kind of attention to detail that made *Billy Elliot* the huge Broadway hit it became.

"It's all about the intention," Mark told me. "You know how to play Billy at eleven. Now just be the same kid two years later."

This changed the show in subtle but powerful ways. For instance, there's a scene where Billy yells at Mrs.

Wilkinson, his dance teacher. Always before, I'd done it like a kid throwing a temper tantrum, but Mark had me tone down the performance so I sounded more like an adult having an argument. It made the show more complex, and deeper emotionally.

Little changes like that helped me continue to fit the part even though I was entering puberty. They also helped keep up my interest. Sometimes, though, I tried to change things on my own, and that never worked out well.

The truth was, I was beginning to worry about my voice. Every singer cracks occasionally, even on Broadway, but soon after the White House event, I started breaking more and more. Some of the big, exciting numbers at the end of Act II were slowly slipping out of my range. David Chase, the show's musical director, rewrote them one by one, bringing down notes, modifying sections, and in some cases, changing the key of the song entirely.

I was going through a big pop music phase at the time, and I noticed something. When all the big divas like Mariah Carey or Christina Aguilera had to hit a really hard high note at the end of a song, they would often riff around it. It's called melisma, in which you sing multiple notes on the same syllable. It allows you hit the note but not have to hold it. One night, I decided to try it myself onstage.

It didn't go over well.

"This isn't a riffing show," said David. "It's not that what you're doing is wrong—you sound great—but that kind of singing is completely different from the rest of the show. It stands out, and not in a good way."

Abashed, I stopped riffing and returned to singing the part as it was written. But what David had said stuck with me. *What I was doing was entirely different from the rest of the show.* For the first time, it made me wonder: if I wanted to do something different, was it time to leave *Billy Elliot* behind?

It was a scary thought, and one I wasn't sure I was ready to contemplate. Counting the auditions, *Billy Elliot* had been part of my life for more than three years. Leaving would mean . . . what? My family had fully transplanted their lives to New York City, and I couldn't see us moving back. Would I go to high school here? Try out for a new show? Get my GED and apply directly to college? I might have been ready to leave *Billy Elliot*, but I wasn't ready to go anywhere else. In the end, I decided to talk to Stephen.

After I explained how I felt, Stephen nodded.

"I'm glad you said something," he said. "This is natural.

There comes a point in every role when you're ready to move on. It's just a matter of doing it the right way. And this is a good time, because your contract's about to be up for renegotiation, and I know you've been having trouble with some of the songs. Maybe it's time for you to leave. You need to think about what you want to do next in life."

"But what if I don't know?" I asked Stephen. I could give him a long list of things I wanted to do with my life in general, but I couldn't say what was *the thing* I wanted to do next.

"What about college?" Stephen asked.

I shook my head no.

"Eventually," I told him. "But I've always been 'the kid' in all my classes. I don't want it to be the same way at college. I want the full experience."

"Well, you should keep dancing," Stephen said. "Take classes at American Ballet Theatre, at least while you figure everything else out. Maybe audition for some acting parts."

It all sounded good, and that was the problem. I couldn't choose one thing over another. Contracts were coming up in a few weeks, and suddenly I felt like everyone was staring at me, wondering what I would do. But a couple of small accidents in a row left the show with a shortage of Billys, and Stephen and the rest of the creative team asked me to stay on for six more months. May 15, 2011, would be my final performance.

After that? I had no clue.

The End

Two weeks before my final show, two very important things happened, one good, one bad. The first was a routine doctor's appointment—or so I thought.

Both of my knees had been bothering me on and off ever since the injury. But in April, my right knee (the one that hadn't torn) became really inflamed. I had to go back to PhysioArts, but after just one session, they sent me to Dr. Hamilton.

"It's just the Osgood-Schlatter stuff, though, right?" I asked him.

"Yes," said Dr. Hamilton. From his tone, though, I knew there was something more. "But it's bad this time. I'm worried you're about to reinjure yourself. I need to take you out of the show for the next few weeks."

"Dr. Hamilton, I'm only *in* the show for two more weeks," I said.

"That's unfortunate, Alex," he replied with a heavy sigh. "But we have to put your health first. I'm sorry, but I can't allow you to perform. I'm taking you out of the show."

I couldn't believe what Dr. Hamilton was saying. After five months of preparing myself to leave in May, had I just been suddenly thrust out the door? Had I already done my last show without even knowing it? I was prepared to leave, but I didn't want to be gone already. I wanted to have my family see my last show, and to say good-bye to my new family from the show. This would be such a letdown. After all the work I'd done, I couldn't believe it was all going to end like this.

No, I decided. *I won't let that happen.*

Panicked and scared, I did the first thing I could think of. I called Mom. Together, we called Stephen.

"He's got to perform," Stephen said as soon as we explained the situation. "Maybe he can take the next month or two off, and then come back for a special return engagement?"

At first, that seemed possible, but the more we thought about it, the less it worked. I would have to remain in rehearsals that entire time, just to keep up to speed. And it would be hard for the rest of the cast and crew to revert to working with me as Billy for just a single performance. No matter how much we tried to justify it, it just didn't make sense.

"What if I take off a few days, and just do my last show?" I said. I could deal with being out a week or two, so long as I could still have that final performance.

"That *could* work . . . ," Stephen replied.

"I sense a 'but' coming," Mom said, when Stephen trailed off.

"*But* you'll need to find a doctor who'll sign you back in. Dr. Hamilton won't. So here's my advice: rest, heal, and get a second opinion."

Rest? Rest was the last thing I wanted. I wanted to make the most of every moment I had left in the show. But Stephen was right. And I already knew the doctor I would go to: Dr. Mysnyk, our old neighbor and Dr. Hamilton's colleague. I'd have to fly back to Iowa, but if it meant I could do my final performance, I'd have *walked* back. That's how much that last show meant to me.

In fact, now that I was at the end of my time in *Billy Elliot*, every performance felt special, and I wished I didn't have to miss a single one. Every time an understudy went on, I thought, *This might be the last time I hear them do this part.* The crew and cast all knew I was leaving, and everyone went out of their way to talk to me, hang out with me backstage, and wish me luck. We really had become like a family. I'd seen these people every day for two years, and now? Now I was leaving, and they all wanted to know where I was headed next.

But I couldn't answer them. I still didn't know what I was doing. I'd figured out certain things: I'd keep studying ballet, probably in the Pre-Professional Division of the Jacqueline Kennedy Onassis School at American Ballet Theatre in the city. But I was going to take a little break first. Since I was out in May (maybe), I could take a month off before starting classes in the summer. My knees, I knew, would thank me for it. I would continue homeschooling and apply to college at the normal age.

"That's a pretty full schedule," Mom said to me. "Maybe that's what you do for the next year."

"Maybe," I said. But it felt like something was missing, like there was something I should be doing, but I just couldn't figure out what it was. I wanted something artistic, but not a show. And I wanted something that felt good, like doing charity events. I wanted to help people, especially kids like me, who had a dream they wanted desperately to fulfill. But I couldn't figure out the right way to do it.

The next day, Mom came home from work at the usual time. I heard her keys in the door and began to pack up my schoolwork so we could get ready for dinner. But then I heard her talking to our neighbor Ellen Stern. Ellen was a writer, and she kept an odd schedule, much like I did, so she'd become close with our family. In fact, whenever Mom went away, Matt and I would spend the night at Ellen's apartment. Whenever we saw her in the hall or elevator, we'd chat for a minute about the show, or the book she was working on. But tonight, she and Mom stood in the hallway talking for nearly twenty minutes, and when Mom came in, she had a thoughtful look on her face.

"What was that about?" I asked her. "Is everything okay with Ellen?"

"Hmm?" Mom said. "Oh, yeah, Ellen's great."

It was clear that Mom was distracted by something. I waited while she puttered around the house, putting her stuff down. Finally, she sat on the couch.

"Alex," she said. "What would you think if I wrote a book?"

"That would be cool," I said. "What kind of book? Like a novel?"

"About you," Mom said. "Or rather, what it takes to raise a successful Broadway actor. It was Ellen's idea. I don't know—she wants me to talk to a friend of hers about it, another writer. Would it be okay if I wrote about you? Would that feel weird?"

I thought about it for a second. There were probably a lot of embarrassing moments in my childhood that I didn't necessarily want the whole world to read about, but aside from that, I actually thought it was kind of cool. I wish we'd had a book like that when I was little, some kind of guide.

"So it would help families like us?"

"Exactly," Mom said. "Normal people with talented kids who want to raise them right."

Mom had never talked about writing before, but I thought it would be great to have an author in the family. I loved writing, and even though dance was my main passion in life, I'd always imagined that I would study writing in college. That's why I wanted to go to Yale, because they had such a strong English department. So I urged Mom to go for it.

Mom met with Ellen's friend, who referred her to an agent named Charlotte Sheedy. A few days later, Charlotte called Mom.

"I love the idea," she said. "And I've seen *Billy Elliot* a dozen times. Alex is incredible."

"Oh, thank you," Mom said. "But I just don't know. I'm not a writer."

"But you have a great idea." Charlotte tried to convince

her. "And the expertise to back it up."

"Maybe. Couldn't someone else write it? Ellen?" Mom sounded uneasy about the idea.

There was a long pause.

"What about Alex?" Charlotte said finally. "Would Alex want to write it?"

"Alex?" Mom said, surprised. "But he's . . . just a kid."

"My daughter wrote a bestseller when she was twelve," Charlotte said. "In fact, it launched her career. You might know her—she's an actress. Ally Sheedy?"

That was enough to convince Mom, who loved *The Breakfast Club*, which was Ally Sheedy's best-known role and one of the movies that had defined the 1980s.

"Would you want to write a book?" Mom asked me that night. "About the show, and how you got on Broadway?"

"I mean, sure, but . . ." I trailed off. Writing seemed like the kind of thing you did when you were older, more experienced, after college at least. I wanted to be a writer someday. But was I ready to be one now? I didn't want to do it unless I knew I could do it well. "Can I do it?"

"Charlotte seems to think so," Mom said. "She wants to meet you. She asked if you were free on . . . oh, wait, I wrote it down somewhere."

Mom rummaged through the papers on the kitchen table.

"Here it is!" She held up a Post-it in triumph. "May sixteenth. Lunch. What do you think?"

May 16. The day after my last show. Suddenly everything clicked. I'd found it, the thing I was supposed to do next. I smiled.

"That sounds great."

But first Mom flew me back to Iowa to have Dr. Mysnyk look at my knee. Michael Kohli was kind enough to look after me while I was there, so Mom didn't have to take time off from work. I got new X-rays, a second MRI, the whole nine yards. In his office, Dr. Mysnyk showed me my file.

"Are you injured?" he said. "Yes."

My heart shrank to about half its size.

"So I can't do my last show?" My voice cracked. This was my last chance, and I'd failed.

Dr. Mysnyk ran his hands through his hair and sighed.

"No," he said. "That's not what I'm saying. Are you injured? Yes. Do I think you should perform anyway? Yes."

"What?" I shot up in surprise.

"You deserve this, Alex. I'm not taking your last show away from you."

He turned to Michael.

"He isn't fully healed, but he should be fine," he said.

"Are you sure?" Michael sounded worried. She knew how much this meant to me, but my health came first.

"If he were my child, I would let him go on. This is a once-in-a-lifetime opportunity, and the chance of any injury is very low. I'm going to give you a topical gel that will help with the pain and the swelling. And after this, you take a break, you hear?"

"Yes, sir!" I said. "Absolutely. That's the plan."

He quickly wrote a prescription on the pad by the desk and tore it off with a flourish.

"Ta-da," he said. "A star is born."

"Thank you, Dr. Mysnyk!" I couldn't stop myself. I leaped out of the chair and ran around to hug him.

"Knock 'em dead," he said.

After that, it was just a matter of waiting. There were only five days left until my final performance. I invited everyone—my family, the friends I'd made in New York, all my mentors and dance teachers throughout the years. Stephen told me he was coming, and so did Kenny Ortega. Mom, Matt, and John would be in the front row. Aunt Pat was flying in, as was Michael Kohli. And Dad would have the best seat in the house.

"So it's almost done," I said to Dad in my prayers the night before my last performance. "I'm almost out of the show. It feels weird to imagine life in New York without it. Isn't that strange, Dad? We live in New York now. I'm a New Yorker. I don't think I'll ever move back to Iowa. I wonder what you'd think of me now."

But I didn't really wonder. I knew. He was proud of me, as proud as he could ever possibly be. When I closed my eyes, I could feel him in the room with me. I could hear his laugh, smell his cooking, feel the sandpaper scruff of his face against mine when we hugged. For just a moment I let myself pretend he was actually with me. I kept my eyes closed tight as I got into bed.

"Good night, Dad. I love you," I whispered to the empty room, which didn't feel empty anymore. Dad was there, in my heart, where he would always be.

Mom took me to the theater that night. When we arrived, she took one look at the big poster of me and started to cry.

"Oh, Alex," she said, pulling me into a hug. "I'm so, so proud of you, honey."

"Mom." I pretended to protest. "I've got a show to do."

She laughed.

"Always the professional," she said. "That's my little boy. Oh! You're not so little now, I guess. Get backstage before I start crying again."

She let me go, but I held on to her hand. Every step of the way, from Iowa to Broadway, Mom had been at my side. She brought me to my first dance class and every gymnastics competition. She stood up for me, fought for me, sacrificed for me. Everything I had done in my life was because of her.

I pulled her hand, bringing her back to me for one more hug.

"I love you, Mom," I whispered.

"I love you too, Alex," she said into my hair. I could hear the excitement in her voice. I squeezed her hard one last time and then ran into the theater, knowing that tonight—like every night—she'd be watching out for me.

The first person to notice me backstage was Kate Dunn. She'd had her baby while I was injured and was back now. As I walked in, she started clapping slowly. Jess, my dresser, joined her. Somehow Stephen was there too, and Joan Lader, and David Chase, and they were all clapping. Soon the whole company was applauding for me, from the ballet girls to the stagehands. We'd put on a show like no other. The men and women in that room had made me a professional and taught me what it meant to be on Broadway. If anyone should have been applauding, it was me. I felt so humbled by the love and support they had shown me.

"How do you feel?" Stephen asked, after the applause died down. I thought about it for a second. How did I feel about tonight? About leaving the show? About everything that came next? I was going to ask what he meant, when I realized that the answer was the same regardless.

"Ready," I said. "I'm ready."

"Good answer." He laughed, and clapped me on the shoulder. "So when do we get to read all about this?"

I'd told Stephen about the book idea, and he was as excited as I was. Billys had gone on to do lots of things, he'd said, but none had written a book about being in the show yet.

"I start tomorrow," I told him. He shook his head with pride.

"Nothing slows you down, does it?" he said admiringly. "Now get out there and show them what you've got!"

He didn't have to tell me twice. Still, I took my time in warm-ups, stretching my knee and making sure I was ready. Truthfully, I wasn't worried, I just wanted to relish the last few moments. *Billy Elliot* had been my first job, my first big role, my first show on Broadway. *Billy Elliot* brought me to New York and sent me to the White House. I'd met celebrities and politicians—and most important, friends I'd have for the rest of my life.

When the call for places came, I started to tear up.

Thankfully, Jess appeared at my side.

"Here," she said, handing me a small pack of Kleenex. "I thought you might need these."

"How do you always know?" I laughed despite my tears.

"That's my job." Jess smiled. "Now it's time for yours. You're great, Alex. Blow them away. We're all rooting for you."

I hugged her and hurried to my mark. The orchestra started and the audience quieted. One by one, members of the ensemble walked past me, just as they had on my first night in the show. Only this time, each of them said good-bye as he walked past, or reached out a hand to shake mine. Soon they were all onstage and I was alone in the dark.

In just a few seconds, it would all start again. My father would grab my hand and drag me out on that stage for the final time. I'd say the words and dance the steps, just like always. It would fly by like lightning and I would remember every second of it in slow motion for the rest of my life.

But tonight would be different.

When I first started the show, I played Billy as a kid: young, innocent, excited. Like he is in the beginning. After my injury, I was more like Billy later in the play: older, experienced, more determined than ever. But tonight I would be neither of those boys.

Instead, I'd play the role a new way: as Billy from the last moment of the show. Billy about to embark on something new, suitcase in hand, staring off into the future, excited and uncertain. Billy on the verge of being a young man.

Tomorrow I'd meet with Charlotte, and a whole new phase of my life would begin. I had no way of knowing what was coming. But I'd learned that we never do, and our uncertainty does nothing to slow life down. It just keeps coming, beautiful and awful and everything, and we make the most of it, because it is a gift from God. *The* gift from God.

In the dark, waiting in the wings, I stood on the threshold between today and tomorrow, between my past and my future. As I waited, I could feel the excitement growing inside me. It was coming. It was coming.

A hand grabbed mine. I closed my eyes.

It was here.

Alex at gymnastics—age 4

Alex and Matt's baptism, 1997

Alex with brothers John and Matt

Sam, Alex, Matt, family friend Alex Wang, and John at RAGBRAI in Coralville, Iowa

Alex and Ming Ming

Alex performing tribute "For Ko Cheuk Man, with Love, from Ko Jun Dak" at the University of Iowa, 2008

Steps on Broadway
(where Alex was discovered)

Celebrating the Billy Elliot *contract signing*

Alex dreams of landing the part of Billy.

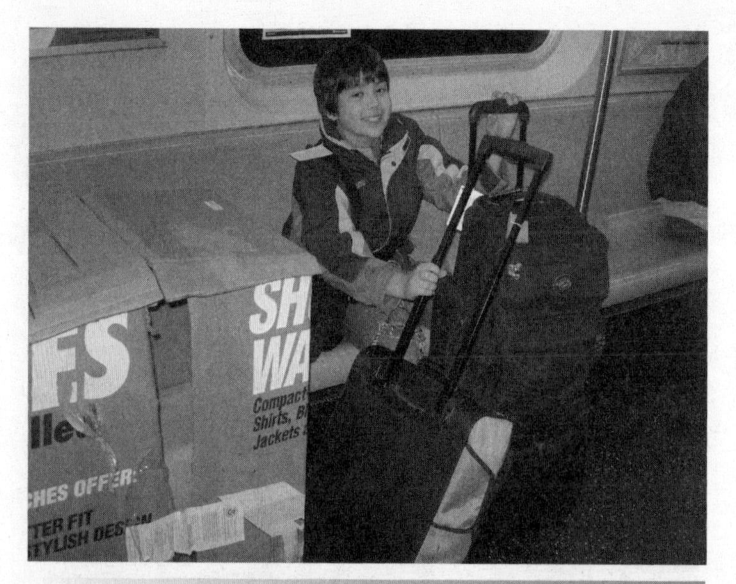

Taking his solo chair packed in the "box of Frankenstein" on the subway

Taking the chair for his solo through Times Square

After auditions!

Performing with actor Gregory Jbara (playing Billy's father)

Alex, Kate Hennig, and the ballet girls performing in Billy Elliot

Alex appears in a Billy Elliot *billboard in Chicago.*

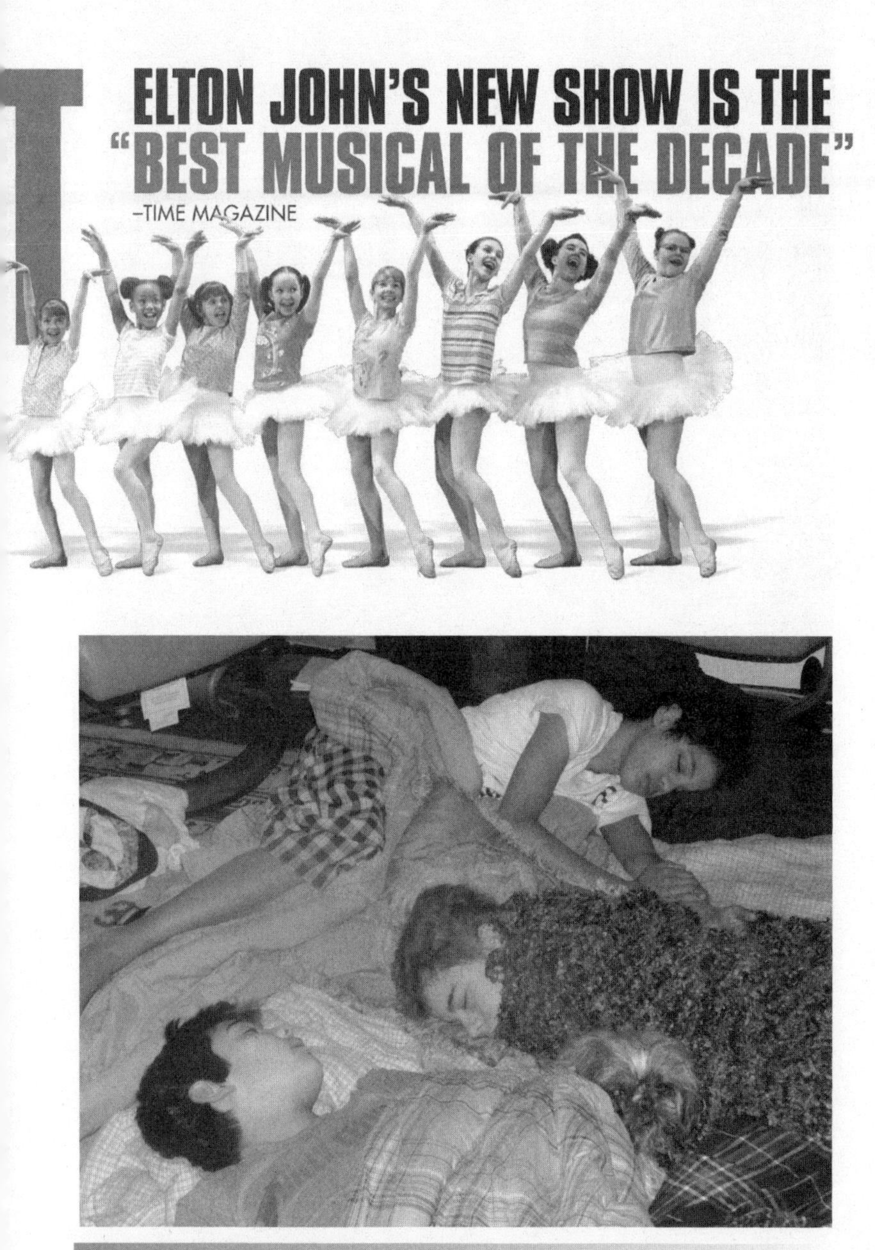

Alex having a sleepover with other Billys, Liam Redhead and Michael Dameski, and dog Ming Ming

With actor Gregory Jbara onstage

Alex and director Stephen Daldry

The presidential seal

Doing arabesques in the White House hallways!

The whole family in California, May 2007

Acknowledgments

First of all, I would like to thank my family, who helped me throughout all the years to get me to where I am. I want to say a special thank-you—and I love you—to my mom, who has always supported me. I couldn't have gone to New York and studied dance at Steps on Broadway if my brother John hadn't worked at the Fareway grocery store to help the family and driven me to my lessons. My brother Matt is always there when I need someone to listen to me about my dreams. My grandma and grandpa have always been proud of me and done what they could. I want to say a special thank-you to Auntie Kristin, Uncle David, Ashleigh, and Alissa for always being supportive, and especially to Auntie Kristin for coming to assist my dad when we needed her in Iowa. Auntie Polly, Auntie Kitty, and Auntie Alicia were really helpful when they came to take care of my dad after the transplant, as were my cousins Emily, Pearl, and David. And Great-grandma, I wish you were still here to see me finish this book.

My dance teachers were so amazing and made this journey possible with the best dance training. I want to thank Michael Kohli from the National Dance Academy for teaching me and being my second mom when I was little. I want to give a big thank-you to Gretchen Steffen from the National Dance Academy for teaching me my very first solo, to "Zip-a-Dee-Doo-Dah." I had the very best duet partner, Peyton McCoy, who made dancing so much fun at the competitions. At the Nolte Academy of Dance, I want to say thank you to Leslie Nolte, Grace Snider, and Tad Snider, who gave me the opportunity to perform in *The Nutcracker*, my first exposure to being in a real ballet. I want to thank Sarah and Eloy Barragan for putting me on a scholarship at City Ballet of Iowa. Eloy was the best ballet mentor and role model when I needed one right after my dad passed away. The tribute Eloy and I created for my dad is something I will treasure forever. I want to thank Marina Trouch and Patty Neuzil for the best costumes that could possibly be made.

My gymnastics coaches were amazing and taught me the value of perseverance, discipline, and being strong. I want to especially thank Dmitri Trouch for training me so well and coaching me to wins and championships. I want to thank Brad Virkler, Linas Gaveika, and Nabil Andrade for their great coaching as well.

I want to say a special thank-you to the best teacher ever, Debbie Wilson. She made me love to learn and helped me become the person I am today. Thank you to the Abdo family for their spiritual support, as well as All Nations Church, Pastor Lee, and Pastor Kung, for teaching us the power of faith and God.

Without Eloy and Michael I would never have been prepared for New York City. In New York, my teachers, Edward Ellison, Fabrice Herrault, Elena Kunikova, and Franco DeVita, helped me improve as an artist. I would not have been Billy on Broadway without the help of Ray Hesselink, Peter O'Brien, and Steps on Broadway, who gave me a scholarship to the summer program. My current ballet mentor, Wilhelm Burmann, is helping me continue with my dream to be the best dancer I can be, and I cannot thank him enough for believing that I could succeed.

Thank you to Brian Gendece, who was an amazing manager and was so supportive in the transition from Iowa to NYC. Thank you is not even enough for Kenny Ortega, who helped me with the many other aspects of being on Broadway. Kenny and his whole family—Dooba, Kyle, Ali, Markie, Shirl, and Manly—are my California family and have been helping me more than I could ever have imagined. And Kelly and Lou Gonda have been amazing and supportive to me and my whole family.

Thank you to Kate Dunn for teaching me to push myself more than I knew I could with my dancing; to Joan Lader for the amazing coaching for my singing; and to Ann Ratray for helping me to be an actor. I want to thank the other Billys I had a chance to work with: Trent, Kiril, David, Tommy, Liam, Dayton, Mike, Jacob, Peter, Joseph, Tade, and Giuseppe. The Billys were supportive of each other and the only others who really understood what it was like to play the role. And thank you to the rest of the *Billy Elliot* cast, guardians, and stage crew for making the show a great family. Without Jessica Scoblick, I would not have been able to perform with the many costume changes. Juliana Hannett helped me with my interviews and not getting nervous before I had to speak. Thank you to Ryan, Liz, Sarah, Suzanne, and Jen at PhysioArts for the best care; and to Dr. Mark Mysnyk, Dr. William Hamilton, and Dr. Phillip Bauman for help with my knees.

There have been many other people who have entered my life since *Billy Elliot* and have continued to support me in a big way, including Lea Salonga. The many dinners at Joe Allen with Farah Fath and John-Paul Lavoisier are some of my favorite memories.

For this book, in particular, I want to thank Charlotte Sheedy for believing in this boy from Iowa who wanted to write a book and taught me how to do the job. I couldn't have had a better editor than Alyson Day at HarperCollins. And thank you to Hugh Ryan for his amazing insights.

As for someone who has done so much for me: I don't know what to say to Stephen Daldry—for believing in me, changing my life, and supporting me in everything I do. You'll be in my life forever.

Finally, I would like to thank my father, whose spirit inspires me to be the best person I can possibly be.